GW01402692

The President's Shadow

Political, Volume 3

Nicholas Andrew Martinez

Published by Harmony House Publishing, 2024.

THE PRESIDENT'S SHADOW

First edition. November 24, 2024.

ISBN: 979-8230998419

Written by Nicholas Andrew Martinez.

Table of Contents

To those who stand in the light to combat the darkness,

To the unsung heroes who defend freedom and justice,

And to my family, whose unwavering support is my constant strength.

This book is for you.

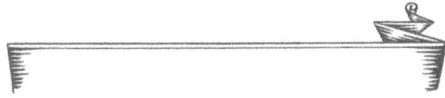

Chapter 1: Inauguration Day

The crisp January air bit at the cheeks of the assembled crowd, a tapestry of patriotic fervor as red, white, and blue flags fluttered in the brisk wind. Washington, D.C., was alive with the buzz of anticipation, the nation's capital transformed into a stage for the grand ceremony. The steps of the Capitol building were a sea of dignitaries, politicians, and citizens alike, all gathered to witness the swearing-in of the 48th President of the United States, Daniel Hayes.

The morning sun cast a golden hue over the scene, reflecting off the marble pillars and lending a sense of timeless grandeur to the event. The air was thick with the hum of conversation, punctuated by the occasional cheer as prominent figures took their seats. Security was tight, with uniformed officers and Secret Service agents strategically positioned, their vigilant eyes scanning the crowd for any sign of trouble.

Daniel Hayes stood backstage, the weight of history and the future pressing down on his shoulders. His hands gripped the podium nervously, feeling the cold metal beneath his fingers. Despite the layers of his tailored suit and overcoat, he felt a chill that had nothing to do with the weather. This was the moment he had worked his entire life for, yet he couldn't shake the gnawing sense of foreboding that lurked in the back of his mind.

"Ready, Mr. President?" a voice asked from behind him. It was Olivia Barnes, his trusted advisor and chief of staff, her expression a mixture of pride and concern.

Hayes turned to face her, offering a small, tight-lipped smile. "As ready as I'll ever be, Olivia."

She nodded, placing a reassuring hand on his arm. "You'll do great. Just remember why you're here and what you stand for."

He took a deep breath, letting her words sink in. This was his moment to lead, to bring the change he had promised to a divided nation. The challenges ahead were immense, but he believed in his vision and the people who had put their faith in him.

The announcer's voice boomed over the loudspeakers, signaling the start of the ceremony. "Ladies and gentlemen, please rise for the oath of office."

The crowd hushed, a wave of silence rolling over them as they stood in unison. Hayes walked out onto the platform, his steps steady and purposeful. The Chief Justice awaited him, holding the Bible upon which he would swear his oath. Hayes met his gaze, drawing strength from the solemnity of the moment.

"Please raise your right hand and repeat after me," the Chief Justice intoned.

Hayes complied, his voice steady and strong as he recited the words that would make him the leader of the free world. "I, Daniel Hayes, do solemnly swear that I will faithfully execute the Office of President of the United States, and will to the best of my ability, preserve, protect, and defend the Constitution of the United States."

The crowd erupted in applause, cheers echoing through the air as Hayes completed the oath. He turned to face them, a broad smile breaking across his face. This was it – the culmination of years of hard work, dedication, and sacrifice. He raised his hands, acknowledging the cheers, feeling a swell of emotion that threatened to overwhelm him.

As the applause died down, Hayes stepped up to the podium to deliver his inaugural address. He looked out over the sea of faces, taking a moment to collect his thoughts. His speech had been carefully crafted, every word chosen to inspire and unite, but now that he stood here, he felt the need to speak from the heart.

"My fellow Americans," he began, his voice carrying across the plaza, "today, we stand at a crossroads in our history. We face unprecedented challenges, both at home and abroad. But with those challenges come opportunities – opportunities to come together, to build a brighter future, and to show the world the true strength of our nation."

He paused, letting the words sink in, watching as the crowd hung on his every word. "I stand before you today, not as a politician, but as a servant of the people. I am here because you believed in me, and I promise to honor that trust.

Together, we will tackle the issues that divide us and work towards a more just, more equitable society."

As he continued his speech, a figure moved quietly through the crowd, unnoticed amidst the sea of faces. The figure was dressed in a plain, unremarkable coat, blending seamlessly with the throng of onlookers. They moved with purpose, eyes fixed on the stage where Hayes stood, a glint of something sinister in their gaze.

Hayes spoke passionately about his vision for the future, touching on themes of unity, progress, and hope. He spoke of the need for bipartisan cooperation, for addressing the deep-seated issues that plagued the nation, and for leading by example on the world stage. The crowd responded enthusiastically, their cheers and applause a testament to their faith in him.

But even as Hayes spoke, the figure in the crowd continued to make their way closer to the stage. They slipped through the barriers, moving with a confidence that suggested they knew exactly where they were going. The figure reached into their coat, fingers brushing against the cold metal of a small device.

As Hayes reached the climax of his speech, urging the nation to come together and rise above their differences, the figure in the crowd activated the device. A soft click, barely audible over the noise of the crowd, signaled the start of a countdown. The figure slipped away, disappearing into the sea of faces as quickly as they had appeared.

"Let us move forward together, as one nation, indivisible, with liberty and justice for all," Hayes concluded, his voice ringing out with conviction.

The crowd erupted in a final, thunderous applause, the sound reverberating through the plaza. Hayes stepped back from the podium, shaking hands with the Chief Justice and other dignitaries. As he turned to leave the stage, Olivia Barnes approached him, her expression troubled.

"Mr. President, we need to move you to a secure location," she said urgently, her voice low.

Hayes frowned, sensing the urgency in her tone. "What's going on, Olivia?"

"We've received a credible threat," she replied, her eyes scanning the crowd. "We need to get you out of here, now."

Hayes nodded, following her lead as they hurried off the stage. The Secret Service agents closed in around them, forming a protective barrier as they made their way to a waiting vehicle. The celebration continued behind them, unaware of the danger that lurked in the shadows.

As the motorcade sped away from the Capitol, Hayes couldn't shake the feeling of unease that had settled over him. The threat, whatever it was, had cast a dark shadow over what should have been a triumphant day. He turned to Olivia, seeking answers.

"What kind of threat are we dealing with?" he asked, his voice tense.

"We're not sure yet," she admitted. "But it was serious enough to warrant immediate action. We're taking every precaution."

Hayes nodded, his mind racing with possibilities. He had known that the road ahead would be difficult, but he hadn't anticipated that the challenges would begin so soon. As the motorcade wound its way through the streets of Washington, he resolved to face whatever lay ahead with the same determination and resolve that had brought him to this point.

The motorcade arrived at a secure location, and Hayes was quickly ushered inside. The room was filled with top advisors, military officials, and intelligence personnel, all gathered to assess the threat. The atmosphere was tense, the gravity of the situation evident on every face.

"Mr. President," General Marcus Lee began, "we received an anonymous tip about a potential attack during the inauguration. We believe it may be linked to a larger conspiracy."

Hayes listened intently, his mind processing the information. "Do we have any leads on who might be behind this?"

"We're still investigating," Lee replied. "But we have reason to believe that it could be the work of a group known as The Shadow Council. They're a highly secretive organization with a history of orchestrating political disruptions."

Olivia Barnes stepped forward, her expression grim. "We've been monitoring their activities for some time, but this is the first indication that they might be targeting the presidency directly."

Hayes felt a surge of anger and determination. He had fought hard to get to this position, and he wasn't about to let some shadowy group undermine his administration. "We need to get to the bottom of this, and fast. I want a full report on The Shadow Council and their activities. And I want our best people on this."

The room buzzed with activity as the various teams sprang into action. Hayes stood at the center, feeling the weight of his new responsibilities pressing down on him. The threats were real, and the challenges immense, but he was resolved to face them head-on.

As the hours passed, Hayes and his team delved deeper into the mysterious threat. They pored over intelligence reports, reviewed security footage, and analyzed every piece of information they could gather. The picture that emerged was troubling – The Shadow Council was a formidable adversary, with resources and connections that spanned the globe.

Despite the seriousness of the situation, Hayes couldn't help but feel a sense of resolve. This was a test, a challenge that he had to meet with strength and determination. He had promised the American people that he would lead them through difficult times, and he intended to keep that promise.

As the day turned into night, Hayes finally took a moment to himself, stepping out onto a balcony to clear his mind. The city stretched out before him, a sea of lights and activity. He took a deep breath, feeling the weight of the presidency settle more firmly on his shoulders.

He knew that the road ahead would be fraught with danger and uncertainty, but he was ready to face it. He was not alone – he had a dedicated team, a nation that believed in him, and a fierce determination to succeed.

The anonymous threat had cast a shadow over his inauguration day, but it had also strengthened his resolve. He would uncover the truth behind The Shadow Council, protect the nation from harm, and lead with the integrity and courage that had brought him to this point.

As he stood there, looking out over the city, Hayes felt a renewed sense of purpose. The journey ahead would be long and difficult, but he was ready to face it. For the sake of the nation, for the people who had placed their trust in him, he would rise to the challenge and prove himself worthy of the office he had sworn to uphold.

The presidency was not just a position of power – it was a responsibility, a calling. And Daniel Hayes was determined to answer that call with everything he had. The shadows might be lurking, but he was ready to face them, to bring light to the darkness, and to lead with unwavering resolve.

As he turned to rejoin his team, Hayes knew that this was just the beginning. The threats were real, but so was his determination. Together, they would face the challenges ahead, and together, they would prevail.

Chapter 2: The Mysterious Letter

President Daniel Hayes had barely settled into the rhythm of his new office when the first sign of trouble emerged. The swearing-in ceremony was still fresh in his mind, but the elation of that moment had given way to the sobering realities of governance. The Oval Office, with its historic grandeur, felt more like a battleground now, with each decision a potential landmine.

It was a chilly Wednesday morning when the letter arrived. Hayes was reviewing intelligence briefs when Olivia Barnes, his chief of staff, entered the room, her expression a mix of confusion and concern.

"Mr. President, this just came in," she said, handing him a plain, unmarked envelope. There was no return address, no indication of its origin. The only distinguishing feature was a wax seal stamped with an unfamiliar emblem.

Hayes frowned, taking the envelope from her. "Where did this come from?"

"One of the Secret Service agents found it slipped under the door to the West Wing," Olivia replied. "It's highly unusual, sir. We've already begun investigating how it got there, but so far, no leads."

Hayes carefully broke the seal and unfolded the letter. His eyes scanned the typed message, his frown deepening with each line:

"Mr. President,

Congratulations on your inauguration. It is a shame that your administration is already under threat. There are forces within your own house conspiring against you. They are closer than you think.

Remember the night in Langley, the promise you made to Sarah? Only someone very close would know.

Trust no one.

Sincerely,

A Friend"

Hayes' heart skipped a beat. The mention of Langley and Sarah was something very few people knew about. It was a private matter, dating back to his time as a congressman when he had worked closely with Sarah Mitchell, a CIA operative, on a highly sensitive operation. That night had been pivotal in his career, and the promise he had made to her was something he had never disclosed, not even to Olivia.

"This... this is serious," Hayes said, looking up at Olivia, his face pale. "Whoever wrote this knows things they shouldn't."

Olivia's eyes widened. "What does it say?"

Hayes handed her the letter. As she read, her expression shifted from curiosity to alarm. "Langley... Sarah... How could anyone know about this? This information is classified."

"That's exactly the point," Hayes replied. "This suggests there's a mole in our midst, someone with access to highly sensitive information."

Olivia nodded, her mind already racing with possibilities. "We need to handle this carefully, sir. If there is a mole, they could be anywhere in the administration."

Hayes leaned back in his chair, the weight of the situation pressing down on him. "We need to keep this between us for now. If word gets out, it could compromise any efforts to find this person."

"Agreed," Olivia said. "I'll start a discreet investigation. We need to look at everyone with access to your personal files and background."

As Olivia left the room, Hayes sat back, staring at the letter in his hands. The implications were chilling. He had always known that his position would come with its share of dangers, but this was different. This was personal, and it struck at the very heart of his administration.

The hours that followed were a blur of meetings and briefings, but the letter remained at the forefront of his mind. Hayes found it difficult to concentrate, the words of the message echoing in his thoughts. He replayed the events of that night in Langley over and over, trying to remember any detail that might offer a clue. But the memory remained stubbornly elusive, and the sense of unease only grew.

By the time evening fell, Hayes was exhausted. He retreated to the private quarters of the White House, seeking a moment of solitude. The grand rooms, filled with history and tradition, offered little comfort. The shadows seemed to press in around him, a reminder of the unseen threats that lurked just beyond the edges of his vision.

He was about to pour himself a drink when there was a knock at the door. It was Olivia, looking as determined as ever.

"We've made some progress," she said, stepping inside. "I've narrowed down the list of people who could have known about Langley and Sarah. It's a short list, but it includes some of your closest advisors."

Hayes nodded, appreciating her thoroughness. "Who's on the list?"

"General Marcus Lee, Secretary of State Thomas Reed, and Sarah Mitchell herself," Olivia said. "All three had access to the information and were involved in some capacity."

Hayes sighed. He trusted all three of them implicitly, but the letter had planted a seed of doubt. "What do we do next?"

"We need to speak with each of them, subtly," Olivia said. "We can't let on that we're investigating. We need to gauge their reactions and see if anything stands out."

Hayes agreed, though the thought of suspecting his closest allies made him uneasy. The next few days were a delicate dance of probing conversations and careful observation. Hayes met with General Lee first, discussing recent security developments. Lee was his usual stoic self, offering no indication that he was anything other than loyal and dedicated.

Next was Thomas Reed, a seasoned politician with a sharp mind. Reed was as polished and composed as ever, discussing foreign policy with a keen intellect. Hayes watched him closely, looking for any sign of deception, but found none.

Finally, there was Sarah Mitchell. Hayes had always admired her sharp wit and unwavering dedication. Their meeting was cordial, with Sarah providing an update on intelligence matters. She was as professional and composed as always, but Hayes couldn't shake the feeling that she was holding something back.

After each meeting, Hayes and Olivia compared notes. Nothing conclusive emerged, but the sense of unease persisted. The more they dug, the more elusive the truth seemed to become.

It was late one evening, a week after the letter had arrived, when a breakthrough came. Hayes was in the Oval Office, reviewing reports, when Olivia burst in, her eyes alight with urgency.

"Mr. President, we found something," she said, her voice breathless.

Hayes looked up, hope and dread mingling in his chest. "What is it?"

Olivia handed him a file. "We intercepted a communication. It's encrypted, but our analysts managed to crack it. It's a message from someone within the administration to an unknown recipient. It mentions Langley and the promise to Sarah."

Hayes felt a surge of adrenaline. "Who sent it?"

Olivia's expression turned grim. "It was traced back to Sarah Mitchell."

Hayes' heart sank. He had trusted Sarah implicitly, but the evidence was damning. He couldn't ignore it. "We need to bring her in. Discreetly."

Olivia nodded. "I'll arrange it."

The next morning, Sarah Mitchell was brought to a secure location for questioning. Hayes and Olivia watched from behind a one-way mirror as agents conducted the interview. Sarah looked composed, but there was a tension in her eyes that hadn't been there before.

"Ms. Mitchell," the lead agent began, "we have reason to believe that you've been communicating with a hostile entity. Do you deny this?"

Sarah's eyes widened, her composure cracking. "I don't know what you're talking about. I've been loyal to this administration and to the president."

The agent produced the intercepted communication. "This message was sent from your terminal. Can you explain that?"

Sarah stared at the document, her face pale. "I didn't send this. Someone must have accessed my terminal. I would never betray the president."

Hayes watched, conflicted. He wanted to believe her, but the evidence was overwhelming. The interview continued, but Sarah maintained her innocence. It was clear she was either a masterful liar or a victim of an elaborate frame-up.

After the interview, Hayes and Olivia discussed their next steps. "What do you think?" Hayes asked, his voice heavy with doubt.

"I don't know," Olivia admitted. "She seemed genuine, but we can't ignore the evidence. We need to dig deeper."

As the investigation continued, Hayes felt the strain of suspicion and mistrust. The administration was on high alert, and every move was scrutinized. The sense of camaraderie that had marked his campaign was eroding, replaced by a pervasive sense of paranoia.

One evening, Hayes was alone in the Oval Office, staring at the mysterious letter. The words seemed to taunt him, a reminder of the unseen enemy that lurked within his own ranks. He was deep in thought when a voice broke the silence.

"Mr. President."

Hayes looked up to see General Marcus Lee standing in the doorway. "General, what brings you here?"

Lee stepped inside, his expression somber. "I've been following the investigation. I think there's something you need to know."

Hayes felt a surge of hope. "What is it?"

Lee took a deep breath. "I've been in contact with a source who has information about The Shadow Council. They claim that Sarah Mitchell is innocent, that she's being framed by someone within our own ranks."

Hayes' heart pounded. "Who?"

Lee's expression was grave. "Secretary of State Thomas Reed."

The revelation hit Hayes like a punch to the gut. Reed had been one of his most trusted advisors, but if what Lee said was true, it meant that the betrayal ran deeper than he had ever imagined.

"We need proof," Hayes said, his mind racing.

Lee nodded. "I've already started gathering evidence. We need to move quickly and carefully. If Reed suspects anything, he could destroy everything."

The next few days were a whirlwind of covert operations and clandestine meetings. Lee's source provided crucial information, linking Reed to The Shadow Council. It was clear that Reed had been orchestrating a campaign of disinformation and sabotage from within the administration.

Hayes felt a mix of anger and betrayal as the pieces fell into place. Reed had been undermining him from the start, using his position to manipulate and deceive. It was a chilling reminder of the lengths some would go to for power.

With the evidence in hand, Hayes and Olivia planned their next move. Reed needed to be confronted and removed from his position, but it had to be done in a way that minimized the fallout. The administration was already under strain, and a scandal could be devastating.

The day of reckoning came sooner than expected. Reed was summoned to a secure meeting room, unaware of what awaited him. Hayes, Olivia, and General Lee were there, along with a team of agents ready to make the arrest.

Reed entered the room, his usual confident demeanor faltering as he took in the scene. "What's going on?" he asked, a hint of unease in his voice.

Hayes stepped forward, holding the evidence. "Thomas, we have reason to believe that you've been working with The Shadow Council. This is your chance to explain yourself."

Reed's face went pale. "I don't know what you're talking about. This is a mistake."

Hayes shook his head. "The evidence is clear. You've been betraying this administration, and you will answer for it."

Reed's eyes darted around the room, realizing there was no escape. He straightened, a cold determination settling over him. "You have no idea what you're dealing with. The Shadow Council is bigger than you can imagine. Removing me won't stop them."

Hayes felt a chill run down his spine. Reed's words were a stark reminder of the broader threat. "We'll deal with that. For now, you're under arrest."

The agents moved in, restraining Reed and leading him away. As the door closed behind him, Hayes felt a mix of relief and apprehension. The immediate threat had been neutralized, but the battle was far from over.

Hayes turned to Olivia and General Lee. "We need to dismantle The Shadow Council and root out any remaining operatives. This is just the beginning."

Olivia nodded, her expression resolute. "We'll find them, sir. We won't let them undermine your administration."

As the investigation continued, Hayes felt a renewed sense of purpose. The mysterious letter had been the catalyst for uncovering a web of deceit, and now, armed with the truth, he was determined to lead with integrity and resolve.

The days ahead would be challenging, but Hayes was ready. He had faced the shadows and emerged stronger, more determined than ever to protect the nation and uphold the values he had sworn to defend.

The presidency was a heavy burden, but Hayes bore it with pride and conviction. With Olivia, General Lee, and his loyal team by his side, he would navigate the treacherous waters of political intrigue and emerge victorious.

As he looked out over the city, Hayes felt a sense of hope. The path ahead was uncertain, but he was ready to face it head-on. The mysterious letter had been a warning, but it had also been a call to action. And Hayes was ready to answer that call with unwavering determination.

Chapter 3: Shadows in the Cabinet

The discovery of Thomas Reed's betrayal sent shockwaves through the White House. President Daniel Hayes had barely had time to process the magnitude of the conspiracy when it became clear that Reed's arrest was just the beginning. The Shadow Council's reach extended deep into the heart of his administration, and rooting out its influence would require careful strategy and unwavering resolve.

Hayes convened a meeting with his most trusted advisor, Olivia Barnes, and General Marcus Lee in the Oval Office. The mood was somber, the air thick with tension. Reed's arrest had been a wake-up call, and now the focus was on identifying any other potential threats within the administration.

"Thomas Reed was a significant player, but he wasn't working alone," Hayes began, his voice steady despite the gravity of the situation. "We need to find out who else is involved and put a stop to this."

Olivia nodded, her expression determined. "I've already started an internal investigation, Mr. President. We'll need to proceed carefully to avoid tipping off any potential conspirators."

General Lee leaned forward, his eyes sharp and focused. "Our best approach is to maintain a low profile while gathering intelligence. We can't afford to make any mistakes."

Hayes agreed. "We need to identify anyone with ties to The Shadow Council and neutralize the threat. Olivia, you'll lead the investigation. I want daily updates on your progress."

Olivia nodded again, already formulating a plan in her mind. "I'll start by reviewing communications and financial records for any suspicious activity. We should also consider polygraph tests for key personnel."

General Lee added, "I'll coordinate with our intelligence agencies to see if we can uncover any external links or suspicious behavior. We need to cover all our bases."

With the plan in place, the team dispersed, each member fully aware of the challenges that lay ahead. The atmosphere within the White House grew increasingly tense as the investigation progressed. Every interaction, every conversation was scrutinized, and trust became a scarce commodity.

Olivia began her work by compiling a list of individuals with access to sensitive information. She focused on those who had close interactions with Reed and those who had shown any unusual behavior in recent months. The list included several high-ranking officials, each of whom had a significant role in the administration.

One of the first names on the list was Secretary of Defense Richard Bennett. Bennett was a seasoned military strategist with a reputation for being meticulous and methodical. He had worked closely with Reed on several key initiatives, and his proximity to the conspiracy made him a person of interest.

Olivia scheduled a discreet meeting with Bennett in her office, ensuring that no one else was aware of the encounter. As Bennett entered the room, Olivia studied him carefully, looking for any sign of guilt or deceit.

"Richard, thank you for coming," Olivia said, motioning for him to take a seat.

Bennett sat down, his expression calm and composed. "Of course, Olivia. What's this about?"

Olivia chose her words carefully. "We're conducting an internal review following Thomas Reed's arrest. Given your close working relationship with him, we need to ask you a few questions."

Bennett's face remained impassive. "I understand. I'm happy to cooperate in any way I can."

Olivia nodded. "Good. Let's start with your recent interactions with Reed. Did you notice anything unusual in his behavior or any conversations that seemed out of place?"

Bennett thought for a moment. "Reed was always very professional, but there were times when he seemed... distracted. I attributed it to the pressures of the job, but in hindsight, there might have been something more."

Olivia made a note of his response. "Did he ever mention The Shadow Council or express any views that aligned with their known objectives?"

Bennett shook his head. "Not to me. But I did notice he had private meetings with a few other officials. I wasn't privy to those discussions."

"Can you provide names?" Olivia asked.

Bennett hesitated. "I'd rather not speculate without concrete evidence, but I can tell you that he often met with Secretary of Commerce Elaine Parker and Chief of Staff Bill Thompson."

Olivia's mind raced. Both Parker and Thompson were influential figures within the administration. If they were involved, the conspiracy could be more extensive than she had initially thought.

"Thank you, Richard," Olivia said. "Your cooperation is appreciated. We'll be in touch if we need any further information."

As Bennett left, Olivia couldn't shake the feeling that he was hiding something. His responses had been measured, almost rehearsed. She made a mental note to have his activities monitored more closely.

Next on her list was Elaine Parker. Parker was known for her sharp intellect and ambitious nature. She had risen through the political ranks quickly, and her position as Secretary of Commerce gave her access to critical economic data and international trade secrets.

Olivia approached Parker with the same level of caution, arranging a private meeting under the pretext of discussing economic policy. Parker arrived at Olivia's office, her demeanor confident and polished.

"Elaine, thank you for meeting with me," Olivia began, offering a warm smile.

"Of course, Olivia. What can I do for you?" Parker replied, her tone friendly but guarded.

"We're reviewing our internal security protocols in light of recent events," Olivia said, choosing her words carefully. "Given your role, I wanted to get your perspective on any potential vulnerabilities."

Parker's eyes narrowed slightly. "I'm always vigilant about security, but Reed's arrest was a shock to all of us. I never suspected he was involved in anything nefarious."

"Did you have any private meetings with Reed in recent months?" Olivia asked, watching Parker's reaction closely.

Parker nodded. "We did discuss several economic initiatives, but nothing out of the ordinary. Our conversations were always focused on policy."

"Did he ever mention any concerns or express views that seemed aligned with external threats?" Olivia probed.

Parker shook her head. "No, he was always very focused on his work. If he had any ulterior motives, he kept them well hidden."

Olivia noted Parker's responses, aware that she needed to tread carefully. "Thank you, Elaine. Your insights are valuable. We'll keep you informed of any developments."

As Parker left, Olivia felt a growing sense of unease. The answers she was getting were too clean, too rehearsed. It was clear that whoever was involved in the conspiracy was skilled at covering their tracks.

The final name on her list was Bill Thompson, the Chief of Staff. Thompson was a seasoned political operative with decades of experience. He had been instrumental in guiding Hayes' campaign and had a reputation for being fiercely loyal.

Olivia decided to approach Thompson more directly, knowing that his reaction would be crucial. She found him in his office, buried in paperwork, and requested a private meeting.

"Bill, we need to talk," Olivia said, closing the door behind her.

Thompson looked up, his expression one of concern. "What's going on, Olivia?"

"We've uncovered evidence that suggests Reed wasn't acting alone," Olivia said bluntly. "I need to know if you've noticed anything suspicious or if you've had any private dealings with him."

Thompson's face tightened. "Are you suggesting I'm involved in this? After all we've been through?"

Olivia held his gaze. "I'm not accusing anyone, Bill. But we need to be thorough. If there's a mole in the administration, we have to find them."

Thompson sighed, leaning back in his chair. "I worked closely with Reed, yes. But I never saw any indication that he was involved in a conspiracy. He was always professional, always focused on his duties."

"Did he ever discuss The Shadow Council with you?" Olivia asked.

Thompson shook his head. "No. And if he had, I would have reported it immediately. My loyalty is to the president and this administration."

Olivia studied him for a moment, sensing his sincerity. "I believe you, Bill. But we have to be sure. I'm going to need access to your communications and financial records, just as a precaution."

Thompson nodded reluctantly. "I understand. Do what you need to do."

As Olivia left Thompson's office, she felt a mix of frustration and determination. The investigation was proving to be more complex than she had anticipated. The suspects were skilled at hiding their tracks, and the lack of concrete evidence made it difficult to make definitive conclusions.

Over the next few days, Olivia and her team conducted a thorough review of communications and financial records. They scrutinized every detail, looking for any anomalies that might point to further involvement in the conspiracy. The process was slow and painstaking, but Olivia knew it was necessary.

During this time, President Hayes maintained a facade of calm and control, but inside, he was deeply troubled. The arrest of Reed had shaken his faith in his team, and the ongoing investigation only added to his anxiety. He trusted Olivia and General Lee implicitly, but the uncertainty gnawed at him.

One evening, as Hayes sat alone in the Oval Office, Olivia entered, her face etched with fatigue.

"We've found something," she said, handing him a report.

Hayes took the report, his heart pounding. "What is it?"

"We've identified several large, unexplained financial transactions linked to Elaine Parker," Olivia said. "The funds were transferred to offshore accounts associated with known members of The Shadow Council."

Hayes felt a surge of anger. "Elaine Parker. I trusted her."

Olivia nodded. "It appears she's been funneling money to The Shadow Council for months. This could be the break we need to unravel the entire conspiracy."

"We need to act quickly," Hayes said, his voice firm. "Bring her in for questioning, and ensure we have enough evidence to detain her."

Olivia left to make the necessary arrangements, and Hayes felt a mix of relief and determination. The investigation was yielding results, and the path to rooting out the conspiracy was becoming clearer.

The following morning, Elaine Parker was brought to a secure location for questioning. Hayes, Olivia, and General Lee watched from behind a one-way mirror as the interrogation began.

"Ms. Parker, we have evidence linking you to The Shadow Council," the lead agent said, placing the financial records on the table. "These transactions are clear indications of your involvement."

Parker's face paled, but she maintained her composure. "I don't know what you're talking about. Those transactions are legitimate business dealings."

"The accounts are linked to known operatives of The Shadow Council," the agent replied. "We have records of your communications with them."

Parker's facade began to crack. "I... I was coerced. They threatened my family. I had no choice."

Hayes felt a surge of anger. "She's lying," he said to Olivia. "She was a willing participant."

Olivia nodded. "We need to get a full confession."

The agent continued to press Parker, her defenses crumbling under the weight of the evidence. Finally, she broke down, admitting her involvement and revealing the names of other operatives within the administration.

Hayes felt a mix of relief and resolve. The web of deceit was unraveling, and with Parker's confession, they had the means to dismantle The Shadow Council's influence.

Over the next few weeks, the administration conducted a series of coordinated arrests, targeting the operatives identified by Parker. The process was arduous and fraught with tension, but each arrest brought them closer to neutralizing the threat.

As the dust settled, Hayes felt a sense of triumph and renewed purpose. The conspiracy had been exposed, and the administration was taking decisive action to restore integrity and trust. The road ahead would still be challenging, but Hayes was more determined than ever to lead with strength and honor.

He convened a meeting with his remaining cabinet members, addressing them with a tone of authority and resolve. "We have faced a grave threat to our administration and our nation," he began. "But we have emerged stronger and more united. Let this be a reminder that we must always remain vigilant and true to our principles. Together, we will continue to lead with integrity and purpose."

The cabinet members nodded, their expressions reflecting a renewed sense of commitment. The shadows that had plagued the administration were dissipating, replaced by a clear vision for the future.

As Hayes looked around the room, he felt a surge of pride and determination. The challenges had been immense, but they had faced them head-on and emerged victorious. The presidency was a heavy burden, but it was one he bore with honor and unwavering resolve.

The investigation had tested the administration's mettle, but it had also forged a stronger, more resilient team. Hayes knew that there would be more challenges ahead, but he was ready to face them with the support of his loyal advisors and the trust of the American people.

The shadows in the cabinet had been exposed and eradicated, and with a renewed sense of purpose, Hayes was ready to lead the nation toward a brighter, more secure future. The journey had been arduous, but it had also been a testament to the strength and resilience of the administration and the principles upon which it stood.

As the meeting concluded, Hayes felt a renewed sense of hope and determination. The road ahead would be challenging, but he was ready to face it with unwavering resolve and the support of his dedicated team. The shadows had been dispelled, and the future was theirs to shape.

With a final look at his cabinet, Hayes spoke with conviction. "Together, we will continue to build a nation that stands for justice, integrity, and unity. The challenges we face will only make us stronger. Let's move forward with determination and resolve, knowing that we are on the right path."

The cabinet members stood, their expressions reflecting a shared sense of purpose. The journey ahead would be long and difficult, but they were ready to face it together, united in their commitment to the nation and its values.

As Hayes left the room, he felt a sense of peace and resolve. The shadows had been dispelled, and the future was bright. The presidency was a heavy burden, but it was one he bore with honor and unwavering resolve. The challenges would continue, but so would their commitment to justice, integrity, and unity.

The administration had been tested and had emerged stronger. The shadows had been exposed, and the light of truth and justice would guide them forward. Hayes was ready to lead with strength and honor, knowing that the future was theirs to shape.

The journey was far from over, but with each step, they would move closer to a brighter, more secure future. The shadows had been dispelled, and the path ahead was clear. Together, they would face the challenges and build a nation that stood for justice, integrity, and unity. The future was bright, and they were ready to face it with unwavering resolve.

Chapter 4: A Blast from the Past

President Daniel Hayes sat in the Oval Office, the weight of recent events pressing heavily on his shoulders. The arrest of Secretary of State Thomas Reed and the subsequent investigation had exposed a conspiracy that threatened the very core of his administration. As he looked out the window at the bustling city of Washington, D.C., he couldn't help but feel a sense of unease. The immediate threat had been neutralized, but he knew that the battle was far from over.

A soft knock on the door brought him out of his reverie. Olivia Barnes, his chief of staff and trusted advisor, entered the room with a clipboard in hand.

"Mr. President, General Marcus Lee is here to see you," she said, her tone professional yet tinged with concern.

Hayes nodded, feeling a surge of anticipation. Marcus Lee was not only one of his most trusted military advisors but also an old friend from his days in the Army. They had served together in some of the most challenging and dangerous missions, and Hayes trusted Lee's judgment implicitly.

"Send him in, Olivia," Hayes replied, standing up and straightening his tie.

A moment later, General Marcus Lee entered the room. He was a tall, imposing figure with a stern demeanor that belied a keen intellect and sharp instincts. His uniform was crisp, and his presence commanded respect.

"Marcus, it's good to see you," Hayes said, extending his hand.

Lee shook his hand firmly. "Good to see you too, Daniel. Though I wish it were under better circumstances."

Hayes gestured for Lee to take a seat. "I appreciate you coming on such short notice. We have a lot to discuss."

Lee nodded, his expression serious. "I've been following the situation closely. Reed's arrest was a significant development, but it's clear that the threat goes much deeper."

Hayes sat back in his chair, feeling the weight of the past few weeks. "You're right. The Shadow Council's influence is more extensive than we initially thought. We need to understand who they are and how to dismantle their network."

Lee leaned forward, his eyes intense. "I've been doing some digging, and I've uncovered some information that might help. The Shadow Council is a secretive group with roots that go back decades. They operate in the shadows, using their influence to manipulate political and economic events to their advantage."

Hayes listened intently, his mind racing with the implications. "Do we know who's behind them?"

Lee shook his head. "Not exactly. They're very good at covering their tracks. But I've managed to identify a few key figures who might be involved. These individuals have connections to both government and private sector entities, making them difficult to pin down."

Hayes felt a mix of frustration and determination. "We need to find a way to expose them. They've already infiltrated my administration, and who knows what else they have planned."

Lee's expression grew even more serious. "There's something else you need to know. The Shadow Council has a history of using extreme measures to achieve their goals. They won't hesitate to use violence or intimidation to silence their enemies."

The gravity of Lee's words settled over Hayes like a heavy blanket. The stakes were higher than ever, and the path ahead was fraught with danger. But Hayes knew that he couldn't back down. The future of his administration—and the nation—depended on their ability to root out this threat.

"Do you have any suggestions on how to proceed?" Hayes asked, his voice steady.

Lee nodded. "We need to approach this from multiple angles. First, we need to gather more intelligence on the key figures involved. I've already started assembling a team of trusted operatives to help with this. Second, we need to tighten security within the administration to prevent further infiltration. And third, we need to find a way to disrupt their operations and cut off their funding sources."

Hayes felt a surge of hope. Lee's plan was sound, and with his expertise and resources, they had a fighting chance. "Let's get started. I want daily updates on our progress. We can't afford any missteps."

Lee stood up, his expression resolute. "We'll get through this, Daniel. We've faced tough challenges before, and we've always come out stronger."

Hayes nodded, feeling a renewed sense of determination. "Thank you, Marcus. I trust you to lead this effort. Together, we'll expose The Shadow Council and protect our nation."

As Lee left the room, Hayes turned to Olivia, who had been quietly observing the conversation. "Olivia, I need you to coordinate with Marcus and provide him with any resources he needs. We're in this together."

Olivia nodded, her eyes reflecting her unwavering commitment. "You can count on me, Mr. President. We'll do whatever it takes to root out this threat."

With a renewed sense of purpose, Hayes returned to his desk. The path ahead would be challenging, but he was ready to face it head-on. The future of his administration—and the nation—depended on their ability to dismantle The Shadow Council and protect the integrity of their democracy.

Over the next few days, the White House became a hive of activity. General Lee's team of operatives, handpicked for their expertise and loyalty, began their investigation in earnest. They worked tirelessly, following leads and uncovering connections that had previously been hidden. Olivia coordinated the efforts, ensuring that every resource was utilized effectively.

The atmosphere within the administration remained tense, with every member of the cabinet under scrutiny. Trust was a rare commodity, and the weight of suspicion hung heavy in the air. Despite the challenges, Hayes felt a growing sense of optimism. They were making progress, and each new piece of information brought them closer to understanding the full extent of The Shadow Council's operations.

One evening, as Hayes was reviewing reports in the Oval Office, Olivia entered with a stack of documents. Her expression was a mix of exhaustion and determination.

"Mr. President, we've made some significant breakthroughs," she said, handing him the documents.

Hayes took the documents and began reading. The information was detailed and comprehensive, outlining the connections between key figures in The Shadow Council and various government and private sector entities. It was clear that their influence extended far beyond the White House.

"This is incredible work, Olivia," Hayes said, feeling a surge of hope. "We're finally starting to see the full picture."

Olivia nodded. "Our operatives have been able to trace several financial transactions that link back to major corporations and political donors. These individuals have been using their influence to manipulate policy decisions and secure lucrative contracts."

Hayes felt a mix of anger and determination. The depth of the corruption was staggering, but he knew that they couldn't afford to let their emotions cloud their judgment. "We need to move quickly and decisively. Have you identified any specific targets we can go after?"

Olivia handed him another document. "We have. There are several high-profile individuals who appear to be key players in The Shadow Council. We're preparing to take action against them, but we need to be careful. They have powerful allies and significant resources."

Hayes reviewed the list of names, recognizing many of them as prominent figures in politics and business. "We'll need to coordinate with law enforcement and intelligence agencies to ensure that we have the evidence to support our actions. I want to make sure that we do this by the book."

Olivia nodded. "I'll start making the necessary arrangements. We'll need to move quickly to prevent any of them from escaping or destroying evidence."

As Olivia left to begin coordinating the operation, Hayes felt a sense of resolve. They were finally making headway, and the prospect of dismantling The Shadow Council's network was within reach. The path ahead would be difficult, but he was ready to face it with the support of his trusted advisors and the unwavering commitment to justice.

The next few days were a whirlwind of activity. General Lee's operatives worked tirelessly to gather the necessary evidence, while Olivia coordinated with law enforcement and intelligence agencies to plan the operation. The atmosphere within the White House was charged with anticipation, as everyone prepared for the decisive action that would take place.

The morning of the operation, Hayes gathered with his key advisors in the Situation Room. The tension was palpable, but there was also a sense of determination. This was the moment they had been working toward, and the success of the operation would be critical in dismantling The Shadow Council's influence.

General Lee stood at the head of the table, outlining the plan. "Our teams are in position, and we have the warrants to arrest the key figures involved. We'll be coordinating with local law enforcement to ensure that everything goes smoothly."

Hayes nodded, feeling a mix of anticipation and resolve. "This is a critical moment for our administration and for the nation. I want to make sure that we do this right. We can't afford any mistakes."

Lee's expression was serious. "We're ready, Mr. President. Our operatives are well-trained and prepared for any contingencies. We'll take these individuals into custody and secure the evidence we need to bring them to justice."

As the operation began, Hayes watched the live feeds from various locations, his heart pounding with anticipation. The teams moved with precision, executing their tasks with professionalism and efficiency. One by one, the key figures involved in The Shadow Council were apprehended, and critical evidence was secured.

The operation was a resounding success, and Hayes felt a surge of relief and pride. The arrests were a significant blow to The Shadow Council, and the evidence gathered would be instrumental in prosecuting those involved. The administration had taken a decisive step in dismantling the conspiracy that had threatened their integrity.

In the days that followed, the arrests made headlines, and the nation watched as the administration took swift and decisive action against the corruption that had infiltrated their ranks. Hayes addressed the nation, his voice steady and resolute.

"Today, we took a significant step in protecting the integrity of our democracy. The arrests and the evidence gathered are a testament to our commitment to justice and the rule of law. We will continue to root out corruption and ensure that those who seek to undermine our nation are held accountable. Together, we will build a future based on integrity, transparency, and unity."

The response from the public was overwhelmingly positive, and Hayes felt a renewed sense of purpose. The battle against The Shadow Council was far from over, but they had made significant progress. The administration had demonstrated its commitment to justice and had taken decisive action to protect the nation.

As Hayes looked out over the city from the balcony of the White House, he felt a sense of pride and resolve. The journey ahead would still be challenging, but he was ready to face it with unwavering determination. With the support of his trusted advisors and the commitment of the American people, they would continue to build a brighter and more secure future.

The presidency was a heavy burden, but it was one that Hayes bore with honor and a deep sense of responsibility. The events of the past weeks had tested their resolve, but they had emerged stronger and more united. The future was theirs to shape, and Hayes was determined to lead with integrity and courage.

With the shadows of The Shadow Council exposed and the path ahead clear, Hayes felt a renewed sense of hope and determination. The challenges would continue, but so would their commitment to justice and the values that defined their nation.

The journey was far from over, but Hayes was ready to face it with the strength and resolve that had brought him to this point. Together, they would build a future based on integrity, transparency, and unity. The future was bright, and they were ready to face it with unwavering determination.

Chapter 5: The Journalist's Scoop

The sun had just begun to rise over Washington, D.C., casting a warm golden hue over the city. The capital, with its historic monuments and bustling streets, seemed to radiate an aura of stability and order. But beneath this facade lay a complex web of power and corruption, one that investigative journalist Sarah Mitchell was determined to unravel.

Sarah had always been driven by a relentless pursuit of the truth. Her career as an investigative journalist had taken her to some of the most dangerous and controversial places in the world, from war-torn regions to the corridors of power in Washington. Her tenacity and unwavering commitment to uncovering the truth had earned her a reputation as one of the best in the field. But her latest investigation promised to be the most challenging and dangerous yet.

It all began with an anonymous tip. A cryptic message delivered to her office in the dead of night, hinting at a vast conspiracy that reached the highest levels of government. The tip had included detailed information about secret meetings, illicit financial transactions, and shadowy figures pulling the strings behind the scenes. Sarah had been skeptical at first, but as she dug deeper, she realized that the evidence was compelling—and terrifying.

Sarah's investigation led her to a series of confidential documents, financial records, and covert communications that pointed to a powerful and secretive group known as The Shadow Council. This group, she discovered, had been manipulating political and economic events for decades, using their influence to control key decisions and amass enormous power. The more she uncovered, the more she realized that the corruption extended far beyond what she had initially imagined.

Her investigation was meticulous and thorough. She spent countless hours poring over documents, interviewing sources, and following leads. She used encrypted communications to protect her sources and ensured that every step of her investigation was conducted with the utmost discretion. The stakes were incredibly high, and Sarah knew that any misstep could not only jeopardize her work but also put her life in danger.

As the evidence mounted, Sarah began to piece together a narrative that was both shocking and disturbing. She discovered that The Shadow Council had infiltrated various branches of government, including the highest levels of the executive branch. They had used their influence to secure lucrative contracts, manipulate elections, and control key policy decisions. The extent of their reach was staggering, and it became clear that they would stop at nothing to maintain their power.

One of the most significant breakthroughs in her investigation came when she uncovered a series of emails and financial transactions linking The Shadow Council to several high-ranking officials in the administration. These officials had received large sums of money in exchange for favorable decisions and had participated in secret meetings to discuss strategy and coordinate their efforts. The evidence was damning, and it confirmed Sarah's worst fears: the corruption reached the very top of the government.

Sarah's investigation took on new urgency when she learned about the threats received by President Hayes. The anonymous threats hinted at a conspiracy within his own administration, and Sarah realized that her findings aligned with these threats. She knew that the president needed to be informed, but she also understood the risks involved. If The Shadow Council learned of her investigation, they would do everything in their power to silence her.

Despite the dangers, Sarah was determined to get the truth out. She decided to reach out to the president directly, using a secure and anonymous channel to share her findings. She compiled a detailed report, including all the evidence she had gathered, and sent it to a trusted contact within the administration. She hoped that President Hayes would take the information seriously and use it to root out the corruption within his ranks.

As she waited for a response, Sarah continued her investigation, uncovering even more evidence of The Shadow Council's activities. She discovered that they had been involved in a wide range of illegal activities, from money laundering and bribery to blackmail and extortion. Their reach extended to the highest levels of government, and their influence was pervasive and insidious.

One of the most shocking revelations came when Sarah uncovered a plot to undermine the president's efforts to dismantle The Shadow Council. The group had planned a series of coordinated attacks, both physical and cyber, to destabilize the administration and protect their interests. The plan was intricate and well-coordinated, and it highlighted the lengths to which The Shadow Council was willing to go to maintain their power.

As the days passed, Sarah's anxiety grew. She knew that time was running out, and she feared that The Shadow Council would discover her investigation before she could get the information to the president. She took every precaution to protect herself, using secure communications and frequently changing locations to avoid detection. But the stress and constant vigilance were taking a toll on her.

Then, one evening, Sarah received a message from her contact within the administration. The president had received her report and was taking the information seriously. He had already begun to take steps to address the corruption within his ranks and had launched an internal investigation to identify and neutralize the members of The Shadow Council. The news was a huge relief to Sarah, and she felt a renewed sense of hope and determination.

But the battle was far from over. Sarah knew that The Shadow Council would not go down without a fight, and she continued her investigation with even greater intensity. She worked tirelessly to uncover more evidence, identify additional members of the group, and expose their activities to the public. The stakes were incredibly high, and the danger was ever-present, but Sarah was determined to see her investigation through to the end.

As she delved deeper into the conspiracy, Sarah uncovered more details about The Shadow Council's operations. She discovered that the group had a complex hierarchy, with key figures overseeing various aspects of their activities. These individuals were highly skilled and experienced, and they operated with a level of secrecy and sophistication that made them difficult to track.

Sarah decided to focus her efforts on identifying and exposing these key figures. She used her network of sources and contacts to gather information and followed every lead with relentless determination. Her investigation led her to several high-profile individuals, including politicians, business leaders, and government officials, all of whom had ties to The Shadow Council.

One of the most significant breakthroughs came when Sarah uncovered a series of financial transactions linking The Shadow Council to a prominent business tycoon named Victor Shaw. Shaw was known for his vast wealth and extensive connections, and he had long been suspected of engaging in shady dealings. Sarah's investigation revealed that Shaw had been using his influence and resources to support The Shadow Council's activities, providing financial backing and facilitating their operations.

Sarah knew that exposing Shaw would be a critical step in dismantling The Shadow Council. She gathered all the evidence she could find, including financial records, emails, and testimonies from sources who had worked with Shaw. She compiled a comprehensive report detailing Shaw's involvement in the conspiracy and prepared to publish her findings.

But before she could go public, Sarah received a chilling warning. An anonymous message appeared in her inbox, threatening her life if she continued her investigation. The message was a stark reminder of the dangers she faced, and it left her feeling shaken and vulnerable. But rather than deterring her, the threat only strengthened her resolve. She knew that she was on the right track, and she was determined to see her investigation through to the end.

Sarah decided to take additional precautions to protect herself. She moved to a secure location and increased her security measures, using encrypted communications and maintaining a low profile. She also reached out to her trusted contacts for support, ensuring that her findings would be published even if something happened to her.

As she continued her investigation, Sarah uncovered even more evidence of The Shadow Council's activities. She discovered that the group had been involved in a wide range of illegal activities, from drug trafficking and arms smuggling to political assassinations and sabotage. Their reach extended far beyond what she had initially imagined, and their influence was pervasive and insidious.

One of the most shocking revelations came when Sarah uncovered a plot to assassinate President Hayes. The plan was intricate and well-coordinated, involving multiple operatives and sophisticated tactics. The goal was to eliminate the president and replace him with a puppet who would be more amenable to The Shadow Council's interests.

Sarah knew that she had to act quickly to prevent the assassination. She contacted her trusted contact within the administration and shared the details of the plot, urging them to take immediate action to protect the president. She also decided to go public with her findings, hoping that the exposure would force The Shadow Council to reconsider their plans.

The response was swift and decisive. The administration launched a major operation to thwart the assassination plot and neutralize the operatives involved. The news of the plot and The Shadow Council's activities made headlines, and the public was outraged by the revelations. The exposure had a significant impact, and it forced The Shadow Council to go into hiding.

But the battle was far from over. Sarah knew that The Shadow Council would regroup and attempt to regain their power. She continued her investigation with even greater intensity, working tirelessly to uncover more evidence and expose the remaining members of the group. The stakes were incredibly high, and the danger was ever-present, but Sarah was determined to see her investigation through to the end.

As the months passed, Sarah's investigation continued to yield significant results. She uncovered more details about The Shadow Council's operations and identified additional members of the group. Her work was instrumental in dismantling the conspiracy and bringing the perpetrators to justice.

President Hayes publicly acknowledged Sarah's contributions, praising her for her courage and determination. He promised to continue the fight against corruption and to ensure that those who sought to undermine the nation's democracy would be held accountable. The administration launched a series of reforms to address the vulnerabilities that had allowed The Shadow Council to operate, and they worked to restore public trust in the government.

Sarah's investigation had far-reaching implications, and it inspired other journalists and investigators to take up the cause. The exposure of The Shadow Council had a ripple effect, leading to further revelations and a broader effort to root out corruption and protect the integrity of the nation's institutions.

For Sarah, the journey had been long and arduous, but it had also been deeply rewarding. She had faced incredible dangers and overcome significant challenges, but her unwavering commitment to the truth had prevailed. Her work had made a lasting impact, and it had reaffirmed her belief in the power of journalism to effect change.

As she looked back on her investigation, Sarah felt a sense of pride and accomplishment. She had uncovered a vast conspiracy and helped to dismantle a powerful and secretive group. Her work had protected the nation and its democracy, and it had shown that even in the face of overwhelming odds, the truth could prevail.

The battle against corruption was far from over, but Sarah was ready to continue the fight. She knew that there would always be those who sought to exploit their power and influence for personal gain, but she also knew that there were people like her who were determined to hold them accountable. The journey ahead would be challenging, but Sarah was ready to face it with unwavering resolve and a steadfast commitment to the truth.

In the end, it was not just the exposure of The Shadow Council that mattered, but the lessons learned and the resolve to prevent such corruption from taking root again. Sarah's work had sparked a movement, one that would continue to shine a light on the darkest corners of power and ensure that the values of justice, integrity, and transparency remained at the heart of the nation's democracy.

The future was uncertain, but with journalists like Sarah Mitchell leading the charge, there was hope that the truth would continue to prevail and that the nation would emerge stronger and more resilient in the face of adversity. The fight for justice and integrity was ongoing, but it was a fight worth waging, and Sarah was ready to continue her mission, one story at a time.

Chapter 6: A Betrayal Unveiled

The tension in the White House had been building for weeks. President Daniel Hayes and his closest advisors were acutely aware that their administration was under siege from within. Despite the successful takedown of several key figures linked to The Shadow Council, the full extent of the conspiracy remained a dark mystery. The stakes could not have been higher, and the sense of urgency pervaded every corner of the administration.

One of the most troubling elements of this crisis was the suspicion that Secretary of State Thomas Reed, one of the president's most trusted cabinet members, was involved. Reed had always been a respected figure, known for his diplomatic acumen and strategic mind. The thought that he could be complicit in such a treacherous scheme was almost unthinkable, but the evidence was mounting.

Olivia Barnes, the president's chief of staff, had been leading a discreet and thorough investigation into Reed's activities. The findings were disturbing. Financial records showed large, unexplained transfers of money linked to offshore accounts. Encrypted communications pointed to secret meetings and discussions with known operatives of The Shadow Council. Despite the damning evidence, they needed more to make a move that could potentially destabilize the administration.

Late one night, as President Hayes sat in the Oval Office reviewing the latest intelligence reports, Olivia walked in with a grim expression on her face. "Mr. President, we have new evidence that confirms our worst fears. Reed is deeply involved with The Shadow Council."

Hayes looked up from his desk, his face a mixture of anger and disappointment. "Tell me everything, Olivia."

She handed him a thick dossier. "Our intelligence team managed to decrypt several communications between Reed and members of The Shadow Council. The messages detail plans to manipulate foreign policy for their benefit and discuss ways to undermine your administration. We also have evidence of financial transactions that link him directly to the group."

Hayes felt a cold knot form in his stomach. Reed had been a trusted advisor, someone he had counted on during some of the most challenging moments of his presidency. "We need to act quickly and decisively," he said, his voice resolute. "We can't afford to let this betrayal go unpunished."

Olivia nodded. "I've already coordinated with the Attorney General and the FBI. We have a plan to arrest Reed discreetly and minimize the fallout. We'll need to brief General Lee and ensure that our security measures are tight. This could have significant repercussions."

As the president and Olivia finalized their plans, the atmosphere in the White House grew increasingly tense. Every member of the administration was on high alert, knowing that a major shakeup was imminent.

The following morning, Reed arrived at the White House for what he believed was a routine cabinet meeting. He was unaware of the storm brewing around him. As he entered the meeting room, he was greeted by the solemn faces of his colleagues. President Hayes stood at the head of the table, his expression cold and determined.

"Thomas, we need to talk," Hayes began, his voice steady but filled with underlying tension. "Please take a seat."

Reed complied, his brow furrowing in confusion. "What's this about, Mr. President?"

Hayes took a deep breath. "We have evidence that you've been working with The Shadow Council to undermine this administration and manipulate foreign policy for your own gain. The evidence is overwhelming."

Reed's face went pale, and he began to protest. "This is outrageous! I've served this administration with loyalty and dedication. These accusations are baseless!"

Olivia stepped forward, holding up the dossier. "We have encrypted communications, financial records, and testimonies from multiple sources. There's no denying your involvement, Thomas."

Reed's expression shifted from shock to anger. "You have no idea what you're dealing with. The Shadow Council is more powerful than you can imagine. You're making a grave mistake."

Hayes remained calm but firm. "We'll take our chances. You're under arrest, Thomas."

As FBI agents entered the room and placed Reed in handcuffs, the gravity of the situation hit everyone present. The arrest of such a high-ranking official was unprecedented and would undoubtedly send shockwaves through the political landscape.

Once Reed was escorted out of the room, Hayes turned to his remaining cabinet members. "This is a dark day for our administration, but it's also a turning point. We must remain vigilant and committed to rooting out this corruption. We will not let The Shadow Council succeed."

The days that followed were a whirlwind of media frenzy and political maneuvering. The news of Reed's arrest dominated the headlines, and the nation watched with bated breath as the administration worked to contain the fallout. President Hayes and his team were inundated with questions from the press, and they had to navigate the delicate balance of transparency and security.

Despite the public spectacle, the internal investigation continued with renewed intensity. Olivia and General Lee led the efforts to dismantle The Shadow Council's network and uncover the full extent of the conspiracy. They knew that Reed's arrest was just the beginning and that there were still many hidden threats to deal with.

In the midst of this chaos, President Hayes received a visit from an unexpected source. Sarah Mitchell, the investigative journalist who had uncovered significant aspects of The Shadow Council's operations, requested a private meeting. Hayes had come to respect her tenacity and courage, and he agreed to meet with her.

Sarah arrived at the White House, her expression determined but anxious. She had more information to share, and she knew that it could be critical in the ongoing investigation. As she sat down with the president in the Oval Office, she laid out her findings.

"Mr. President, I've continued my investigation, and I've uncovered more about The Shadow Council's operations," she began. "There are several high-profile individuals involved, including foreign agents and powerful business figures. Their influence extends far beyond what we initially thought."

Hayes listened intently, his mind racing with the implications. "What have you found, Sarah?"

She handed him a stack of documents. "These are financial records and communications that link key figures in the business world to The Shadow Council. They've been using their wealth and connections to manipulate markets and political decisions. They have a network of operatives across the globe, and they're deeply embedded in various sectors."

Hayes felt a surge of determination. "We need to act on this information immediately. This is a global threat, and we can't afford to let them continue their operations."

Sarah nodded. "I've also identified several potential targets for further investigation. We need to expose these individuals and cut off their resources. It won't be easy, but it's the only way to dismantle The Shadow Council."

Hayes agreed. "We'll coordinate with our international allies and launch a comprehensive operation to take down these operatives. Your work has been invaluable, Sarah. We couldn't have gotten this far without you."

As the meeting concluded, Hayes felt a renewed sense of hope. The fight against The Shadow Council was far from over, but they were making significant progress. The administration was committed to rooting out corruption and protecting the integrity of the nation.

In the weeks that followed, the administration launched a series of coordinated operations to target The Shadow Council's operatives and cut off their resources. The efforts were intensive and required collaboration with international intelligence agencies and law enforcement. The scope of the conspiracy was staggering, but with each successful operation, they inched closer to dismantling the network.

President Hayes and his team remained vigilant, knowing that the battle was far from over. The threat posed by The Shadow Council was pervasive and insidious, and they had to remain focused and determined. The stakes were incredibly high, but Hayes was resolute in his commitment to justice and integrity.

Throughout this tumultuous period, the support and loyalty of his team were crucial. Olivia Barnes continued to coordinate the investigation with unwavering dedication, and General Lee provided invaluable strategic guidance. Together, they navigated the complexities of the situation and worked tirelessly to protect the administration and the nation.

The arrest of Thomas Reed had been a turning point, but it was also a stark reminder of the challenges they faced. The Shadow Council was a formidable adversary, and they would stop at nothing to maintain their power. But with each step, Hayes and his team grew stronger and more determined.

As the months passed, the administration made significant strides in dismantling The Shadow Council's network. High-profile arrests were made, and critical operations were disrupted. The public watched with a mix of relief and anticipation as the administration took decisive action to protect the nation.

In the end, it was a combination of tenacity, courage, and strategic brilliance that led to the downfall of The Shadow Council. The administration's efforts were recognized and celebrated, and President Hayes emerged as a symbol of integrity and resilience.

The journey had been long and arduous, but the fight against corruption and betrayal had been worth it. The administration had faced incredible challenges and had emerged stronger and more united. The future was uncertain, but with the unwavering commitment to justice and the support of a dedicated team, President Hayes was ready to continue leading the nation with honor and integrity.

As he looked out over the city from the balcony of the White House, Hayes felt a sense of pride and determination. The shadows of The Shadow Council had been exposed and eradicated, and the path ahead was clear. Together, they had faced the darkness and emerged victorious, and the future was bright with the promise of justice and integrity.

The presidency was a heavy burden, but it was one that Hayes bore with honor and a deep sense of responsibility. The challenges had been immense, but they had demonstrated their commitment to justice and the values that defined their nation. The journey was far from over, but with each step, they moved closer to building a brighter and more secure future.

The betrayal had been unveiled, and the fight against corruption continued. But with the strength and resolve of President Hayes and his team, the nation was in capable hands. The future was theirs to shape, and they were ready to face it with unwavering determination and a steadfast commitment to justice.

Chapter 7: The Hidden Agenda

The White House was enveloped in a sense of quiet tension. The recent arrest of Thomas Reed had sent shockwaves through the administration, but President Daniel Hayes knew that their fight against The Shadow Council was far from over. Each day seemed to bring new revelations, deepening the complexity of the conspiracy and underscoring the pervasive threat that loomed over his administration.

The early morning light streamed through the windows of the Oval Office as Hayes sat at his desk, reviewing the latest intelligence reports. His mind was focused on the daunting task ahead—dismantling a shadowy network that had infiltrated the highest levels of government. As he pored over the documents, a sense of unease settled over him. The more he uncovered, the more he realized that the scope of the conspiracy was far greater than he had initially imagined.

A soft knock on the door brought him out of his thoughts. Olivia Barnes, his chief of staff, entered the room, her expression serious.

"Mr. President, we have a situation," she said, handing him a classified dossier. "Our intelligence team has uncovered evidence that The Shadow Council has infiltrated multiple government agencies. The extent of their reach is staggering."

Hayes took the dossier, his heart pounding as he opened it. The documents detailed a series of covert operations and communications that revealed the depth of The Shadow Council's infiltration. They had operatives embedded in key positions within the FBI, CIA, Department of Defense, and even the Treasury. These operatives had been using their positions to manipulate decisions, gather intelligence, and sabotage efforts to root out corruption.

"This is worse than I thought," Hayes said, his voice tinged with frustration. "We knew they were powerful, but this level of infiltration is unprecedented."

Olivia nodded. "We're dealing with a highly organized and well-funded network. They've been operating in the shadows for years, slowly expanding their influence. We need to take broader action to address this threat."

Hayes leaned back in his chair, his mind racing with the implications. "We need to overhaul our entire approach. This isn't just about removing a few bad actors; we need to cleanse our agencies from the inside out. But how do we do that without causing mass panic or tipping off the operatives?"

Olivia's expression was resolute. "We need to start with a thorough vetting process for all high-level positions. Anyone with even a hint of suspicion needs to be investigated. We'll also need to implement more stringent security protocols and enhance our counterintelligence efforts."

Hayes nodded. "And we'll need to do this quietly. If The Shadow Council realizes we're onto them, they'll go underground and it will be even harder to root them out. We need to strike swiftly and decisively."

The president called a meeting with his top advisors, including General Marcus Lee and Attorney General Rachel Martinez. The mood in the Situation Room was tense as Hayes outlined the gravity of the situation.

"We're facing an unprecedented threat," Hayes began, his voice steady but urgent. "The Shadow Council has infiltrated multiple government agencies, and their operatives are embedded in key positions. We need to act quickly and decisively to root out this corruption."

General Lee's expression was grim. "We'll need to conduct a thorough audit of all personnel and operations. This will require coordination with all intelligence and law enforcement agencies. It's a massive undertaking, but it's the only way to ensure we eliminate the threat."

Attorney General Martinez added, "We'll need to secure all communications and ensure that our investigative efforts are not compromised. This will require top-level secrecy and coordination."

The team worked late into the night, developing a comprehensive plan to address the infiltration. They devised a multi-pronged strategy that included enhanced security measures, covert investigations, and coordinated operations to identify and neutralize The Shadow Council's operatives. The plan also involved increasing cybersecurity efforts to protect against further infiltration and sabotage.

As the days turned into weeks, the administration began to implement their plan. The process was slow and meticulous, requiring careful coordination and unwavering vigilance. The team knew that any misstep could compromise their efforts and allow The Shadow Council to regroup.

The first step was to conduct a thorough vetting of all high-level personnel. This involved reviewing backgrounds, financial records, and communications for any signs of suspicious activity. The process was exhaustive and required the cooperation of multiple agencies.

During this time, President Hayes received regular updates from Olivia and General Lee. Each new piece of information added to the growing picture of The Shadow Council's operations. The scale of the infiltration was staggering, and the team realized that they were dealing with a highly sophisticated adversary.

One evening, as Hayes sat in the Oval Office reviewing the latest reports, Olivia entered the room with a look of urgency.

"Mr. President, we've uncovered something significant," she said, handing him a classified document. "Our investigators have identified a high-ranking operative within the CIA. He's been feeding information to The Shadow Council for years."

Hayes took the document and scanned it quickly. The operative, identified as Deputy Director Robert Stanton, had been using his position to gather intelligence and manipulate operations to benefit The Shadow Council. The evidence was clear and damning.

"We need to move quickly to apprehend him," Hayes said. "But we also need to ensure that we gather as much intelligence as possible before making the arrest. We need to understand the full extent of his activities and connections."

Olivia nodded. "We've already started monitoring his communications and movements. We're also coordinating with our international allies to track any interactions he may have had with foreign operatives."

The arrest of Deputy Director Stanton was a significant breakthrough in the investigation. The intelligence gathered from his communications provided valuable insights into The Shadow Council's operations and revealed additional operatives within various government agencies.

As the investigation continued, the administration made a series of high-profile arrests, each one bringing them closer to dismantling The Shadow Council's network. The process was slow and arduous, but the team remained focused and determined.

Throughout this challenging period, President Hayes maintained a steady hand, guiding his administration with resolve and clarity. He knew that the fight against The Shadow Council was far from over, but each step brought them closer to achieving their goal.

One of the most significant challenges was addressing the public's growing concern about the infiltration. The administration had to balance transparency with the need for secrecy, ensuring that their efforts were not compromised while maintaining public trust.

Hayes decided to address the nation in a televised speech, outlining the gravity of the situation and the steps being taken to address the threat. As he stood before the cameras, he spoke with conviction and determination.

"My fellow Americans, we are facing an unprecedented threat to our democracy. A shadowy network has infiltrated multiple government agencies, seeking to manipulate and undermine our institutions. But let me be clear: we will not allow this to continue. We are taking decisive action to root out this corruption and protect the integrity of our government. Together, we will overcome this challenge and emerge stronger and more united."

The response from the public was overwhelmingly supportive, and Hayes felt a renewed sense of purpose. The fight against The Shadow Council was difficult and dangerous, but it was also a testament to the resilience and determination of the nation.

As the months passed, the administration made significant progress in dismantling The Shadow Council's network. High-profile arrests were made, and critical operations were disrupted. The team's efforts were recognized and celebrated, and President Hayes emerged as a symbol of integrity and resilience.

Throughout this tumultuous period, the support and loyalty of his team were crucial. Olivia Barnes continued to coordinate the investigation with unwavering dedication, and General Lee provided invaluable strategic guidance. Together, they navigated the complexities of the situation and worked tirelessly to protect the administration and the nation.

One evening, as Hayes sat in the Oval Office reflecting on the progress they had made, Olivia entered with a look of satisfaction.

"Mr. President, we've just received confirmation that our latest operation was a success," she said. "We've managed to apprehend several key figures within The Shadow Council, and we've secured critical evidence that will help us dismantle their network completely."

Hayes felt a surge of relief and pride. "This is a significant victory, Olivia. We've come a long way, but the fight isn't over yet. We need to remain vigilant and ensure that we continue to protect our institutions."

Olivia nodded. "Absolutely, Mr. President. We'll continue our efforts and work to prevent any future infiltration. The resilience and dedication of this administration will ensure that we prevail."

As the weeks turned into months, the administration's efforts to root out The Shadow Council's operatives continued to yield significant results. The public watched with a mix of relief and anticipation as the administration took decisive action to protect the nation.

The journey had been long and arduous, but the fight against corruption and betrayal had been worth it. The administration had faced incredible challenges and had emerged stronger and more united. The future was uncertain, but with the unwavering commitment to justice and the support of a dedicated team, President Hayes was ready to continue leading the nation with honor and integrity.

As he looked out over the city from the balcony of the White House, Hayes felt a sense of pride and determination. The shadows of The Shadow Council had been exposed and eradicated, and the path ahead was clear. Together, they had faced the darkness and emerged victorious, and the future was bright with the promise of justice and integrity.

The presidency was a heavy burden, but it was one that Hayes bore with honor and a deep sense of responsibility. The challenges had been immense, but they had demonstrated their commitment to justice and the values that defined their nation. The journey was far from over, but with each step, they moved closer to building a brighter and more secure future.

As the administration continued to make progress in dismantling The Shadow Council's network, Hayes knew that the fight against corruption would be an ongoing battle. But with the strength and resolve of his team, he was confident that they would continue to protect the integrity of the nation's institutions.

The betrayal had been unveiled, and the fight against corruption continued. But with the strength and resolve of President Hayes and his team, the nation was in capable hands. The future was theirs to shape, and they were ready to face it with unwavering determination and a steadfast commitment to justice.

Chapter 8: The Underground Network

The lights of Washington, D.C. glimmered against the night sky as Olivia Barnes and General Marcus Lee walked briskly down a dimly lit hallway within a secure government building. The air was thick with anticipation and urgency, knowing that the fate of the administration—and perhaps the nation—depended on the success of their next move.

President Hayes had given them his full support to set up a covert operation aimed at dismantling The Shadow Council once and for all. The threat had grown too great, the infiltration too deep, to rely solely on traditional methods. They needed to gather crucial information quickly and decisively, and to do so, they would need to operate in the shadows, just like their adversaries.

Olivia and General Lee had called this meeting in utmost secrecy, enlisting the help of former intelligence officers and hackers known for their skills and loyalty. The room they entered was equipped with the latest in surveillance countermeasures, ensuring that no prying eyes or ears would compromise their mission.

As they stepped inside, they were greeted by a group of individuals who had dedicated their lives to national security but had long since left the official corridors of power. These were men and women who understood the stakes and the need for discretion. Among them was John Carter, a former CIA operative with a reputation for his undercover work, and Rachel Wu, a cybersecurity expert and hacker extraordinaire whose skills were unmatched in the digital realm.

"Thank you all for coming," Olivia began, her voice firm but earnest. "We are facing an unprecedented threat. The Shadow Council has infiltrated multiple government agencies, and their influence extends far beyond what we initially thought. We need to dismantle their network, and we need your help to do it."

General Lee stepped forward, his presence commanding the room. "We have evidence that The Shadow Council is not only manipulating political decisions but also controlling significant financial resources. Their operations are highly sophisticated and well-hidden. Our objective is to identify their key operatives, gather actionable intelligence, and disrupt their activities."

John Carter, the seasoned CIA operative, nodded thoughtfully. "We've faced shadowy networks before, but this one sounds exceptionally dangerous. What kind of resources and support are we looking at?"

Olivia replied, "You'll have the full backing of the administration, but this operation must remain covert. We can't afford to tip them off. We'll provide whatever you need in terms of equipment and support, but operational security is paramount."

Rachel Wu, the cybersecurity expert, spoke next. "We'll need to establish a secure communication network, using encrypted channels that are completely off the grid. We also need to gather as much digital intel as possible. Their financial transactions, communications, anything that can give us a lead."

General Lee agreed. "We're counting on you to penetrate their digital defenses, Rachel. Your skills will be crucial in identifying their network and tracing their operations back to their sources."

With the objectives laid out, the team began to formulate their plan. The first step was to establish a base of operations that would serve as their command center. They chose a nondescript building in a quiet neighborhood, outfitting it with state-of-the-art surveillance and communication technology. This would be their war room, where they would coordinate their efforts and analyze the intelligence they gathered.

The next phase involved deploying field operatives to gather human intelligence. John Carter led a team of former intelligence officers who would infiltrate circles suspected of harboring Shadow Council operatives. They adopted various covers, posing as businesspeople, lobbyists, and other influential figures to gain access to critical information.

Meanwhile, Rachel Wu and her team of hackers set to work on the digital front. They used sophisticated hacking tools and techniques to breach secure networks, monitor communications, and trace financial transactions. The information they uncovered was fed back to the command center, where it was analyzed and cross-referenced with the intelligence gathered by the field operatives.

As the days turned into weeks, the operation began to yield significant results. The team identified several key operatives within The Shadow Council, uncovering a web of connections that spanned across multiple sectors. They discovered that the network was using shell companies and offshore accounts to launder money and finance their operations. These financial channels were crucial to their power, and disrupting them would be a major blow.

One evening, as the team convened in the command center to review their progress, Olivia addressed the group. "We've made significant headway, but we're only scratching the surface. We need to go deeper, identify their leaders, and understand their ultimate goals. This isn't just about taking down a few operatives; we need to dismantle the entire network."

General Lee added, "Our next step is to disrupt their financial operations. Rachel, we'll need you to lead a cyber operation to freeze their accounts and trace the funds back to their sources. John, your team will need to coordinate with our international partners to conduct simultaneous raids on their financial hubs."

Rachel nodded, already formulating a plan in her mind. "We'll need to move quickly and decisively. Once we start freezing their assets, they'll know we're onto them. We need to be ready to strike at all their key locations at once."

John Carter, the experienced field operative, agreed. "We'll coordinate with international law enforcement to ensure that we have the manpower and resources to hit all their targets simultaneously. Timing will be critical."

With the plan set, the team sprang into action. Rachel and her hackers launched a coordinated cyber attack on The Shadow Council's financial networks, breaching their defenses and freezing their accounts. They traced the funds back to their sources, uncovering a network of shell companies and offshore accounts.

Simultaneously, John Carter's team, working with international partners, conducted raids on key financial hubs, seizing documents and evidence that further exposed the network's operations. The raids were executed with precision, and the team managed to apprehend several high-ranking operatives.

The operation was a resounding success, but it also triggered a swift and deadly response from The Shadow Council. They retaliated with a series of cyber attacks and coordinated efforts to discredit and intimidate the operatives involved in the operation. The team had anticipated this, and they had measures in place to protect themselves, but the intensity of the retaliation underscored the ruthlessness of their adversary.

In the days that followed, the command center became a hive of activity. The team worked around the clock to analyze the intelligence they had gathered, identifying more operatives and tracing the network's operations to their sources. The information they uncovered was crucial, but it also revealed the full extent of the threat they were facing.

One evening, as Olivia and General Lee reviewed the latest reports, Rachel Wu entered the room with a look of urgency. "We've uncovered something significant," she said, placing a set of documents on the table. "The Shadow Council has been using a sophisticated AI system to coordinate their operations and manage their communications. It's highly advanced, and it's allowing them to stay one step ahead of us."

General Lee leaned forward, studying the documents. "This AI system could be the key to their entire operation. If we can take it down, we can disrupt their communications and coordination."

Olivia nodded. "We need to launch a cyber operation to neutralize this AI system. Rachel, you'll lead the effort. We'll also need to deploy field operatives to secure any physical infrastructure associated with the system."

The operation to neutralize the AI system was one of the most challenging and complex undertakings the team had faced. Rachel and her hackers developed a sophisticated cyber attack, using advanced techniques to breach the system's defenses. They faced intense resistance, but their expertise and determination prevailed.

Meanwhile, John Carter's team conducted a series of coordinated raids on facilities suspected of housing the AI system's physical infrastructure. The raids were executed with precision, and the team managed to secure critical components of the system, further crippling The Shadow Council's operations.

The success of the operation was a major blow to The Shadow Council, but it also triggered a desperate and dangerous response. The network's leaders, realizing the severity of the threat, began to take increasingly drastic measures to protect themselves and their operations. The team had to remain vigilant and prepared for any contingency.

As the weeks passed, the team continued to make significant progress in dismantling The Shadow Council's network. They identified more operatives, disrupted key operations, and gathered critical intelligence that further exposed the network's activities. The combined efforts of the field operatives and hackers were instrumental in weakening the network's hold.

One evening, as the team gathered in the command center to review their progress, Olivia addressed the group. "We've made incredible strides, but our work isn't done. We need to continue our efforts and remain vigilant. The Shadow Council is a formidable adversary, but we have the skills and determination to see this through."

General Lee added, "We've dealt them a significant blow, but we need to remain focused. Our objective is to dismantle their network completely and ensure that they can't regroup. We're in this for the long haul, and we need to be prepared for any challenges that come our way."

The team's efforts were recognized and celebrated, and the administration's commitment to rooting out corruption and protecting the nation's institutions was reaffirmed. President Hayes publicly acknowledged the team's contributions, praising their courage and determination.

Throughout this tumultuous period, the support and loyalty of the team were crucial. Olivia Barnes continued to coordinate the operation with unwavering dedication, and General Lee provided invaluable strategic guidance. Together, they navigated the complexities of the situation and worked tirelessly to protect the administration and the nation.

As the months passed, the administration's efforts to dismantle The Shadow Council's network continued to yield significant results. The public watched with a mix of relief and anticipation as the administration took decisive action to protect the nation.

In the end, it was a combination of tenacity, courage, and strategic brilliance that led to the downfall of The Shadow Council. The administration's efforts were recognized and celebrated, and President Hayes emerged as a symbol of integrity and resilience.

The journey had been long and arduous, but the fight against corruption and betrayal had been worth it. The administration had faced incredible challenges and had emerged stronger and more united. The future was uncertain, but with the unwavering commitment to justice and the support of a dedicated team, President Hayes was ready to continue leading the nation with honor and integrity.

As he looked out over the city from the balcony of the White House, Hayes felt a sense of pride and determination. The shadows of The Shadow Council had been exposed and eradicated, and the path ahead was clear. Together, they had faced the darkness and emerged victorious, and the future was bright with the promise of justice and integrity.

The presidency was a heavy burden, but it was one that Hayes bore with honor and a deep sense of responsibility. The challenges had been immense, but they had demonstrated their commitment to justice and the values that defined their nation. The journey was far from over, but with each step, they moved closer to building a brighter and more secure future.

The betrayal had been unveiled, and the fight against corruption continued. But with the strength and resolve of President Hayes and his team, the nation was in capable hands. The future was theirs to shape, and they were ready to face it with unwavering determination and a steadfast commitment to justice.

One particular operation exemplified the complexity and danger of their mission. As the team gathered intelligence on a key figure within The Shadow Council, they discovered that he was planning a major operation that could destabilize the government. The target was a high-ranking official who had been instrumental in the administration's efforts to combat corruption.

The team quickly devised a plan to intercept the operation and apprehend the key figure. The mission required a coordinated effort between field operatives and hackers, with John Carter and Rachel Wu leading their respective teams.

The night of the operation was tense and filled with anticipation. John's team infiltrated the target location, using their skills and training to avoid detection. Meanwhile, Rachel and her hackers monitored communications and provided real-time intelligence to the field operatives.

As John's team closed in on the target, they encountered unexpected resistance. The Shadow Council had anticipated their move and had deployed heavily armed guards to protect their operative. A fierce firefight ensued, with both sides exchanging gunfire in the dimly lit warehouse.

John's team fought with determination, using their tactical training to outmaneuver the guards. They managed to breach the inner sanctum of the warehouse, where they found the key figure surrounded by a group of loyal operatives.

"Drop your weapons!" John commanded, his voice echoing through the room.

The key figure, a middle-aged man with a cold, calculating demeanor, smiled mockingly. "You have no idea what you're up against," he said. "The Shadow Council is far more powerful than you can imagine."

John remained resolute. "We'll see about that. You're coming with us."

As the operatives secured the key figure, Rachel's team detected a sudden spike in communications activity. The Shadow Council was mobilizing their resources, preparing for a counterattack to rescue their captured leader.

"John, we've got company!" Rachel warned over the secure comms. "They're sending reinforcements to your location. You need to get out of there now!"

John's team quickly extracted the key figure and made their way to the exit. The reinforcements arrived just as they were leaving, but John's team managed to escape under the cover of darkness, with the captured operative in tow.

The successful capture of the key figure was a significant victory, but it also highlighted the danger and complexity of their mission. The team interrogated the captured operative, extracting valuable intelligence that further exposed The Shadow Council's operations and plans.

The information they gathered revealed a network of safe houses, financial channels, and communication hubs used by The Shadow Council. The team quickly moved to disrupt these operations, conducting a series of raids and cyber attacks that crippled the network's infrastructure.

The administration's efforts were relentless, and the cumulative impact of their operations began to take a toll on The Shadow Council. The network's leaders were forced to go into hiding, their resources depleted, and their communications disrupted.

As the team continued their efforts, they uncovered a plan by The Shadow Council to launch a major cyber attack on critical government infrastructure. The plan involved using a sophisticated virus to disable communication networks, power grids, and financial systems, causing widespread chaos and undermining public confidence in the government.

Rachel and her team of hackers worked tirelessly to neutralize the threat. They developed a counter-virus and deployed it to the targeted systems, effectively neutralizing the attack and ensuring the security of the nation's infrastructure.

The success of the operation was a testament to the team's skill and determination. They had faced a formidable adversary and had emerged victorious, protecting the nation from a potentially devastating attack.

As the months passed, the administration's efforts to dismantle The Shadow Council's network continued to yield significant results. The public watched with a mix of relief and anticipation as the administration took decisive action to protect the nation.

The journey had been long and arduous, but the fight against corruption and betrayal had been worth it. The administration had faced incredible challenges and had emerged stronger and more united. The future was uncertain, but with the unwavering commitment to justice and the support of a dedicated team, President Hayes was ready to continue leading the nation with honor and integrity.

As he looked out over the city from the balcony of the White House, Hayes felt a sense of pride and determination. The shadows of The Shadow Council had been exposed and eradicated, and the path ahead was clear. Together, they had faced the darkness and emerged victorious, and the future was bright with the promise of justice and integrity.

The presidency was a heavy burden, but it was one that Hayes bore with honor and a deep sense of responsibility. The challenges had been immense, but they had demonstrated their commitment to justice and the values that defined their nation. The journey was far from over, but with each step, they moved closer to building a brighter and more secure future.

The betrayal had been unveiled, and the fight against corruption continued. But with the strength and resolve of President Hayes and his team, the nation was in capable hands. The future was theirs to shape, and they were ready to face it with unwavering determination and a steadfast commitment to justice.

Chapter 9: The Unseen Enemy

Washington, D.C. awoke to an eerie stillness. The usually bustling streets and offices were subdued, the air heavy with an unspoken tension. President Daniel Hayes and his administration had spent months fighting The Shadow Council, making significant strides in dismantling their underground network. However, an uneasy calm had settled over the capital, a calm that felt like the breath before a storm.

In the heart of the White House, the Situation Room was a hive of activity. Olivia Barnes, the president's chief of staff, stood before a large screen, displaying a map of the city with blinking red indicators showing the areas affected by the latest developments. General Marcus Lee and other top advisors were gathered around the table, their faces set with determination and concern.

"We've confirmed multiple cyberattacks targeting key infrastructure," Olivia began, her voice steady despite the gravity of the situation. "The Shadow Council has launched a coordinated offensive against our communication networks, financial systems, and power grids. The attacks are sophisticated and widespread."

General Lee nodded, his expression grim. "Our cybersecurity teams are working around the clock to mitigate the damage, but the scale of the attacks is unprecedented. We're dealing with a highly organized and well-funded enemy."

President Hayes listened intently, his mind racing with the implications. "What about our countermeasures? How effective have they been?"

Rachel Wu, the cybersecurity expert who had been instrumental in their previous operations, spoke up. "We've managed to neutralize some of the attacks, but they keep evolving. It's clear that The Shadow Council anticipated our defenses and adapted accordingly. They're using advanced AI algorithms to coordinate their efforts, making it difficult to predict their next move."

Hayes felt a knot of frustration and determination form in his chest. "We need to stay one step ahead. Increase our cybersecurity efforts and ensure that all critical systems are protected. We can't afford to let them cripple our infrastructure."

As the team continued to strategize, the scale of the chaos outside the White House became more apparent. The cyberattacks had caused widespread disruptions, with power outages affecting large swathes of the city, financial transactions grinding to a halt, and communication networks faltering. The public, already on edge from the recent revelations of corruption, was growing increasingly anxious and distrustful.

In addition to the cyberattacks, The Shadow Council had launched a sophisticated disinformation campaign aimed at further eroding public trust in the government. Social media platforms were flooded with false information and incendiary rhetoric, sowing confusion and fear among the populace. The coordinated effort was designed to undermine the administration's credibility and destabilize the nation.

As President Hayes addressed the nation from the Oval Office, his voice was calm but resolute. "My fellow Americans, we are facing a coordinated attack on our nation's infrastructure and our very way of life. The Shadow Council is using cyberattacks and disinformation to create chaos and undermine our government. But let me be clear: we will not be intimidated. We are taking every measure to protect our systems and ensure your safety. We will emerge from this stronger and more united."

Despite his assurances, the impact of the attacks was profound. Public trust in the government continued to erode, with many people questioning the administration's ability to protect the nation. The streets of Washington, D.C. were filled with protests and demonstrations, the atmosphere charged with anger and uncertainty.

Amidst the chaos, Olivia and General Lee intensified their efforts to identify and neutralize The Shadow Council's operatives. They enlisted the help of former intelligence officers and cybersecurity experts, working tirelessly to trace the origins of the cyberattacks and dismantle the network responsible.

One evening, as Olivia reviewed the latest intelligence reports in her office, she received an urgent call from Rachel Wu. "Olivia, we've detected a new wave of attacks. This time, they're targeting our financial institutions and critical infrastructure simultaneously. It's a full-scale assault."

Olivia's heart raced as she absorbed the news. "We need to act quickly. Coordinate with General Lee and get our response teams mobilized. We can't let them succeed."

Rachel's voice was tense but focused. "Understood. I'll have my team on it immediately."

As the night wore on, the situation grew increasingly dire. The coordinated cyberattacks were relentless, causing widespread disruptions and economic turmoil. Banks and financial institutions were hit hard, with transactions being blocked and records being tampered with. The stock market experienced wild fluctuations, further fueling public anxiety.

At the same time, power grids were targeted, leading to blackouts in several major cities. Emergency services struggled to respond to the crises, and the strain on resources was palpable. The Shadow Council's disinformation campaign added to the chaos, spreading false reports and conspiracy theories that exacerbated the public's fears.

In the White House, the Situation Room was a flurry of activity. President Hayes, Olivia, General Lee, and their top advisors worked tirelessly to coordinate the response. The stakes had never been higher, and every decision was critical.

"We need to focus on stabilizing the financial sector first," General Lee said, his voice steady but urgent. "If we can restore confidence in the markets, it will go a long way in calming the public."

Rachel Wu nodded in agreement. "Our cybersecurity teams are working to secure the financial networks, but we need to communicate clearly with the public to counter the disinformation."

President Hayes turned to Olivia. "Prepare a statement for me. I need to address the nation again, reassure them that we're taking control of the situation."

Olivia quickly drafted a statement, emphasizing the administration's efforts to counter the attacks and protect the nation. Hayes delivered the address from the Oval Office, his tone firm and reassuring.

"My fellow Americans, we are facing an unprecedented attack on our financial institutions and critical infrastructure. Rest assured, we are taking every measure to protect our systems and restore stability. Our cybersecurity teams are working around the clock to neutralize these threats, and we are coordinating with financial institutions to ensure the integrity of our markets. Together, we will overcome this challenge."

The president's address helped to calm some of the immediate fears, but the situation remained volatile. The administration continued to work tirelessly to mitigate the damage and restore order, but the scope of the attacks was immense.

In the days that followed, the team intensified their efforts to trace the origins of the cyberattacks. Rachel Wu and her hackers used advanced techniques to penetrate the digital defenses of The Shadow Council, uncovering critical information about their operations.

One breakthrough came when they identified a series of encrypted communications between key operatives. The messages revealed a coordinated effort to destabilize the government and create chaos, with detailed plans for future attacks. The intelligence was invaluable, providing the administration with a clearer picture of the enemy's capabilities and intentions.

Armed with this information, Olivia and General Lee devised a plan to strike back. They coordinated with international partners to conduct simultaneous raids on The Shadow Council's key facilities, disrupting their operations and apprehending several high-ranking operatives.

The raids were a significant success, but they also revealed the true extent of the network's reach. The captured operatives provided valuable intelligence, but they also confirmed that The Shadow Council had deeply embedded operatives in critical positions across multiple sectors.

As the administration continued its efforts to dismantle the network, public trust remained fragile. The disinformation campaign had sown deep seeds of doubt, and the cyberattacks had exposed vulnerabilities in the nation's infrastructure. The administration faced an uphill battle to restore confidence and ensure the nation's security.

President Hayes knew that their fight against The Shadow Council was far from over. The enemy was cunning and resilient, and they would stop at nothing to achieve their goals. But he also knew that they had the skills and determination to prevail.

One evening, as Hayes sat in the Oval Office reflecting on the challenges they faced, Olivia entered with a determined look on her face.

"Mr. President, we've made significant progress in tracing the origins of the cyberattacks," she said, handing him a report. "We've identified several key operatives and their locations. We're planning a coordinated operation to apprehend them and disrupt their activities."

Hayes nodded, feeling a surge of determination. "Good work, Olivia. We need to keep the pressure on them. Every step we take brings us closer to dismantling their network."

The operation was meticulously planned and executed. Rachel Wu and her team launched a series of cyberattacks to disrupt The Shadow Council's communications and coordination, while John Carter and his field operatives conducted raids on key locations. The operation was a success, resulting in the capture of several high-ranking operatives and the seizure of critical intelligence.

The captured operatives provided valuable information, revealing more about The Shadow Council's operations and plans. The administration used this intelligence to launch further operations, disrupting key activities and weakening the network's hold.

Despite the successes, the fight was far from over. The Shadow Council continued to adapt and evolve, using their resources and influence to mount new attacks and spread disinformation. The administration had to remain vigilant and proactive, constantly adjusting their strategies to stay ahead of the enemy.

As the weeks passed, the team's efforts began to yield significant results. The public started to see the administration's determination and resilience, and confidence slowly began to return. The stock market stabilized, and financial institutions resumed normal operations. Power grids were secured, and communication networks were restored.

President Hayes addressed the nation once again, his tone resolute and hopeful. "My fellow Americans, we have faced an unprecedented challenge, but we have stood strong. Our efforts to dismantle The Shadow Council's network are yielding results, and we are restoring stability and security. We will continue to fight for the integrity of our nation and the trust of our people. Together, we will emerge from this stronger and more united."

The administration's efforts were recognized and celebrated, and President Hayes emerged as a symbol of integrity and resilience. The fight against The Shadow Council had tested their resolve, but it had also strengthened their commitment to justice and the values that defined their nation.

As the administration continued its efforts to protect the nation and restore public trust, President Hayes knew that the journey was far from over. The fight against corruption and betrayal would be ongoing, but with the support of a dedicated team and the determination to see it through, they would prevail.

The shadows of The Shadow Council had been exposed, and the path ahead was clear. Together, they had faced the darkness and emerged victorious, and the future was bright with the promise of justice and integrity.

The presidency was a heavy burden, but it was one that Hayes bore with honor and a deep sense of responsibility. The challenges had been immense, but they had demonstrated their commitment to justice and the values that defined their nation. The journey was far from over, but with each step, they moved closer to building a brighter and more secure future.

The betrayal had been unveiled, and the fight against corruption continued. But with the strength and resolve of President Hayes and his team, the nation was in capable hands. The future was theirs to shape, and they were ready to face it with unwavering determination and a steadfast commitment to justice.

As the administration continued to make progress in dismantling The Shadow Council's network, they remained vigilant and proactive. The enemy was cunning and resilient, but the administration's determination and resolve were unwavering.

One evening, as President Hayes sat in the Oval Office reflecting on the progress they had made, Olivia entered with a determined look on her face.

"Mr. President, we've identified another key operative within The Shadow Council," she said, handing him a report. "This operative has been coordinating the disinformation campaign and is responsible for many of the cyberattacks we've faced."

Hayes felt a surge of determination. "We need to take them down. What's the plan?"

Olivia outlined the operation, which involved a coordinated effort between cyber operatives and field agents. Rachel Wu would lead the cyber aspect, using advanced techniques to breach the operative's digital defenses and gather critical intelligence. John Carter's team would handle the physical apprehension, conducting a raid to capture the operative and secure any evidence.

The operation was meticulously planned and executed. Rachel's team launched a cyberattack to disrupt the operative's communications and coordination, while John's team moved in to apprehend the target. The raid was a success, resulting in the capture of the operative and the seizure of critical evidence.

The captured operative provided valuable intelligence, revealing more about The Shadow Council's operations and plans. The administration used this intelligence to launch further operations, disrupting key activities and weakening the network's hold.

Despite the successes, the fight was far from over. The Shadow Council continued to adapt and evolve, using their resources and influence to mount new attacks and spread disinformation. The administration had to remain vigilant and proactive, constantly adjusting their strategies to stay ahead of the enemy.

As the weeks passed, the team's efforts began to yield significant results. The public started to see the administration's determination and resilience, and confidence slowly began to return. The stock market stabilized, and financial institutions resumed normal operations. Power grids were secured, and communication networks were restored.

President Hayes addressed the nation once again, his tone resolute and hopeful. "My fellow Americans, we have faced an unprecedented challenge, but we have stood strong. Our efforts to dismantle The Shadow Council's network are yielding results, and we are restoring stability and security. We will continue to fight for the integrity of our nation and the trust of our people. Together, we will emerge from this stronger and more united."

The administration's efforts were recognized and celebrated, and President Hayes emerged as a symbol of integrity and resilience. The fight against The Shadow Council had tested their resolve, but it had also strengthened their commitment to justice and the values that defined their nation.

As the administration continued its efforts to protect the nation and restore public trust, President Hayes knew that the journey was far from over.

The fight against corruption and betrayal would be ongoing, but with the support of a dedicated team and the determination to see it through, they would prevail.

The shadows of The Shadow Council had been exposed, and the path ahead was clear. Together, they had faced the darkness and emerged victorious, and the future was bright with the promise of justice and integrity.

The presidency was a heavy burden, but it was one that Hayes bore with honor and a deep sense of responsibility. The challenges had been immense, but they had demonstrated their commitment to justice and the values that defined their nation. The journey was far from over, but with each step, they moved closer to building a brighter and more secure future.

The betrayal had been unveiled, and the fight against corruption continued. But with the strength and resolve of President Hayes and his team, the nation was in capable hands. The future was theirs to shape, and they were ready to face it with unwavering determination and a steadfast commitment to justice.

Chapter 10: The Secret Meeting

The air was thick with anticipation as President Daniel Hayes prepared for one of the most critical meetings of his presidency. The Shadow Council's infiltration and attacks had revealed the terrifying scope of their influence, not just within the United States, but across the globe. The realization that this shadowy network operated internationally and posed a global threat had prompted Hayes to take unprecedented action. Today, he would meet with foreign leaders to discuss forming an alliance against their common enemy.

The secret meeting was set to take place in a secure location in Geneva, Switzerland. This neutral ground had been chosen to ensure the utmost discretion and security. The logistics of arranging such a meeting were complex, with security details, encrypted communications, and covert travel arrangements all meticulously planned to prevent any leaks or interference.

As Air Force One descended into Geneva, Hayes felt the weight of the moment. The world was watching, though few knew the full extent of the crisis they faced. The leaders he was about to meet were all well aware of the stakes. They represented countries that had also felt the sting of The Shadow Council's manipulations and attacks, and they knew that failure to address this threat could have catastrophic consequences.

The convoy of black SUVs moved swiftly and quietly through the streets of Geneva, arriving at a secluded estate surrounded by high walls and dense foliage. The estate was heavily guarded, with security personnel stationed at every entrance. The leaders were ushered into a grand, yet austere meeting room, its large windows offering a view of the serene Swiss countryside—a stark contrast to the tense atmosphere inside.

President Hayes entered the room to find the other leaders already gathered: Prime Minister Emily Lang of the United Kingdom, President

Jean-Luc Dubois of France, Chancellor Anke Müller of Germany, and President Yukio Tanaka of Japan. Each leader brought with them a team of top advisors and intelligence officials. The room buzzed with hushed conversations and the occasional glance at the clock, a testament to the urgency and gravity of the meeting.

Hayes took his seat at the round table, acknowledging each leader with a nod. "Thank you all for coming," he began, his voice steady and authoritative. "We face an unprecedented threat in The Shadow Council. Their reach is global, and their actions have already caused significant harm to our nations. Today, we must form an alliance to combat this common enemy."

Prime Minister Lang was the first to respond. "President Hayes, the United Kingdom has also been targeted by The Shadow Council. Our intelligence agencies have uncovered numerous plots aimed at destabilizing our government and economy. We agree that a coordinated response is essential."

President Dubois of France added, "The attacks in France have been relentless. Our financial institutions, infrastructure, and even our electoral processes have been compromised. The Shadow Council's influence is insidious, and we cannot defeat them alone."

Chancellor Müller nodded in agreement. "Germany has experienced similar threats. Our cybersecurity teams have been working tirelessly to counter the attacks, but it's clear that The Shadow Council's resources and capabilities are vast. We need to share intelligence and resources to effectively combat this threat."

President Tanaka spoke next. "Japan has also been a target. Our technological and industrial sectors have been particularly affected. The Shadow Council's tactics are sophisticated and ruthless. We must stand together to protect our nations."

Hayes listened intently, recognizing the commonality of their experiences. "Our intelligence has revealed that The Shadow Council operates through a network of operatives embedded in key positions within our governments, financial institutions, and other critical sectors. Their goal is to manipulate and control for their gain. We need to share our intelligence, coordinate our efforts, and strike at the heart of their operations."

The leaders discussed the specifics of their cooperation. They agreed to establish a joint task force composed of top intelligence and cybersecurity experts from each nation. This task force would share intelligence, conduct coordinated operations, and develop strategies to counter The Shadow Council's tactics. The alliance would also involve regular communication and collaboration at the highest levels of government.

As the discussions progressed, it became clear that while they all shared a common goal, there were also underlying tensions and differing priorities. Each leader had their own domestic concerns and political pressures, and balancing these with the need for international cooperation was a delicate task.

Prime Minister Lang raised a concern. "While we are committed to this alliance, we must ensure that our national security and sovereignty are respected. Our citizens need to know that we are acting in their best interests."

Chancellor Müller agreed. "Transparency with our citizens is crucial. We must find a way to balance our covert operations with maintaining public trust."

President Dubois added, "We must also be mindful of the potential for The Shadow Council to exploit any perceived weaknesses in our alliance. We need to present a united front and avoid giving them any opportunity to drive wedges between us."

President Tanaka spoke thoughtfully. "Our cooperation must be built on mutual trust and respect. We need to ensure that our intelligence sharing is comprehensive and timely, and that we support each other in both offensive and defensive operations."

Hayes acknowledged their concerns. "You're right. This alliance must be strong and resilient. We need to establish clear protocols for intelligence sharing, joint operations, and communication. We also need to prepare for the possibility that The Shadow Council will attempt to retaliate and undermine our efforts. We must remain vigilant and adaptable."

As the leaders continued to discuss the logistics and strategies of their alliance, a sense of cautious optimism began to emerge. They knew that the road ahead would be challenging, but there was also a shared determination to confront and defeat The Shadow Council.

The meeting concluded with a formal agreement to establish the joint task force and a commitment to ongoing collaboration. The leaders exchanged contact information for their top intelligence officials and set a date for the first task force meeting.

As President Hayes prepared to leave the estate, he felt a mix of relief and resolve. The formation of this alliance was a critical step forward, but it was only the beginning. The fight against The Shadow Council would require sustained effort, cooperation, and resilience.

Back in Washington, D.C., Hayes briefed his top advisors on the outcomes of the meeting. Olivia Barnes, General Marcus Lee, and Rachel Wu listened intently as Hayes outlined the agreement and the next steps.

"We have the support of our international partners," Hayes said. "The joint task force will be crucial in coordinating our efforts and sharing intelligence. We need to ensure that our teams are ready to collaborate effectively and that we maintain the highest levels of security and discretion."

Olivia nodded. "I'll coordinate with our intelligence agencies to prepare for the task force meeting. We need to establish secure communication channels and ensure that our operatives are fully briefed and ready to work with our international counterparts."

General Lee added, "We'll also need to develop joint operational plans. Our military and cybersecurity teams must be prepared to conduct coordinated strikes and defenses. This will require extensive planning and training."

Rachel Wu spoke up. "The cybersecurity aspect will be critical. We need to integrate our digital defenses and offensive capabilities with those of our allies. I'll work with their cybersecurity experts to develop a comprehensive strategy."

As the administration began to implement the plans for the alliance, the scale and complexity of the task became apparent. The joint task force faced numerous challenges, from integrating diverse intelligence and cybersecurity systems to navigating the political dynamics of international cooperation.

The first meeting of the joint task force took place in a secure facility in London. Representatives from the United States, United Kingdom, France, Germany, and Japan gathered to discuss their strategy and coordinate their efforts. The atmosphere was one of cautious optimism, with a clear understanding of the gravity of their mission.

John Carter, the experienced CIA operative, led the U.S. delegation. His expertise in undercover operations and intelligence gathering was invaluable, and he quickly established a rapport with his international counterparts. Rachel Wu and her team of hackers worked closely with cybersecurity experts from the other nations, developing a unified digital defense and offensive strategy.

The task force established a secure communication network, using encrypted channels to share intelligence and coordinate operations. They developed joint operational plans, identifying key targets within The Shadow Council's network and planning coordinated strikes to disrupt their activities.

As the task force began to execute their plans, they faced numerous challenges. The Shadow Council was highly adaptive and resilient, constantly evolving their tactics to counter the task force's efforts. The operatives within the task force had to remain vigilant and proactive, anticipating the enemy's moves and staying one step ahead.

One of the most significant operations involved a coordinated raid on a major financial hub used by The Shadow Council to launder money and fund their activities. The intelligence gathered by the task force revealed the location of the hub, and a detailed plan was developed to strike simultaneously in multiple countries.

The operation was meticulously planned, with teams from each nation coordinating their efforts to ensure a successful outcome. The raid was executed with precision, resulting in the capture of several high-ranking operatives and the seizure of critical financial records and assets.

The success of the operation was a major blow to The Shadow Council, disrupting their financial operations and weakening their ability to fund their activities. The intelligence gathered from the captured operatives provided valuable insights into the network's operations and plans.

Despite the successes, the task force faced ongoing challenges. The Shadow Council continued to adapt and evolve, using their resources and influence to mount new attacks and spread disinformation. The task force had to remain vigilant and proactive, constantly adjusting their strategies to stay ahead of the enemy.

As the months passed, the task force's efforts began to yield significant results. The public started to see the determination and resilience of the international alliance, and confidence slowly began to return. The stock markets stabilized, financial institutions resumed normal operations, and critical infrastructure was secured.

President Hayes addressed the nation once again, his tone resolute and hopeful. "My fellow Americans, we have faced an unprecedented challenge, but we have stood strong. Our international alliance is yielding results, and we are restoring stability and security. We will continue to fight for the integrity of our nation and the trust of our people. Together, we will emerge from this stronger and more united."

The administration's efforts were recognized and celebrated, and President Hayes emerged as a symbol of integrity and resilience. The fight against The Shadow Council had tested their resolve, but it had also strengthened their commitment to justice and the values that defined their nation.

Throughout this tumultuous period, the support and loyalty of the task force were crucial. Olivia Barnes continued to coordinate the operation with unwavering dedication, and General Lee provided invaluable strategic guidance. Together, they navigated the complexities of the situation and worked tirelessly to protect the administration and the nation.

One evening, as President Hayes sat in the Oval Office reflecting on the progress they had made, Olivia entered with a determined look on her face.

"Mr. President, we've identified another key operative within The Shadow Council," she said, handing him a report. "This operative has been coordinating the disinformation campaign and is responsible for many of the cyberattacks we've faced."

Hayes felt a surge of determination. "We need to take them down. What's the plan?"

Olivia outlined the operation, which involved a coordinated effort between cyber operatives and field agents. Rachel Wu would lead the cyber aspect, using advanced techniques to breach the operative's digital defenses and gather critical intelligence. John Carter's team would handle the physical apprehension, conducting a raid to capture the operative and secure any evidence.

The operation was meticulously planned and executed. Rachel's team launched a cyberattack to disrupt the operative's communications and coordination, while John's team moved in to apprehend the target. The raid was a success, resulting in the capture of the operative and the seizure of critical evidence.

The captured operative provided valuable intelligence, revealing more about The Shadow Council's operations and plans. The administration used this intelligence to launch further operations, disrupting key activities and weakening the network's hold.

Despite the successes, the fight was far from over. The Shadow Council continued to adapt and evolve, using their resources and influence to mount new attacks and spread disinformation. The administration had to remain vigilant and proactive, constantly adjusting their strategies to stay ahead of the enemy.

As the weeks passed, the team's efforts began to yield significant results. The public started to see the administration's determination and resilience, and confidence slowly began to return. The stock market stabilized, and financial institutions resumed normal operations. Power grids were secured, and communication networks were restored.

President Hayes addressed the nation once again, his tone resolute and hopeful. "My fellow Americans, we have faced an unprecedented challenge, but we have stood strong. Our efforts to dismantle The Shadow Council's network are yielding results, and we are restoring stability and security. We will continue to fight for the integrity of our nation and the trust of our people. Together, we will emerge from this stronger and more united."

The administration's efforts were recognized and celebrated, and President Hayes emerged as a symbol of integrity and resilience. The fight against The Shadow Council had tested their resolve, but it had also strengthened their commitment to justice and the values that defined their nation.

As the administration continued its efforts to protect the nation and restore public trust, President Hayes knew that the journey was far from over. The fight against corruption and betrayal would be ongoing, but with the support of a dedicated team and the determination to see it through, they would prevail.

The shadows of The Shadow Council had been exposed, and the path ahead was clear. Together, they had faced the darkness and emerged victorious, and the future was bright with the promise of justice and integrity.

The presidency was a heavy burden, but it was one that Hayes bore with honor and a deep sense of responsibility. The challenges had been immense, but they had demonstrated their commitment to justice and the values that defined their nation. The journey was far from over, but with each step, they moved closer to building a brighter and more secure future.

The betrayal had been unveiled, and the fight against corruption continued. But with the strength and resolve of President Hayes and his team, the nation was in capable hands. The future was theirs to shape, and they were ready to face it with unwavering determination and a steadfast commitment to justice.

Chapter 11: The Assassination Attempt

The day began like any other for President Daniel Hayes. He had an early morning briefing with his national security team, followed by a meeting with economic advisors to discuss ongoing efforts to stabilize the financial sector after the recent cyberattacks. Despite the intense pressure of his role, Hayes approached his duties with a calm and resolute demeanor, knowing that the nation depended on his leadership.

However, beneath the veneer of routine, there was an undercurrent of tension. The Shadow Council, their grip weakened but not broken, had been growing increasingly desperate. Their latest moves had been bold and aggressive, a sign that they were willing to take drastic measures to maintain their power. As Hayes went about his day, he was unaware that a plot was unfolding that would shake the nation to its core.

It was mid-morning when Hayes left the White House to attend a scheduled public event—a speech at the National Press Club where he planned to address the recent successes in combating The Shadow Council and outline the administration's next steps. The motorcade moved smoothly through the streets of Washington, D.C., with the Secret Service maintaining a vigilant watch over every detail of the journey.

The venue was filled with journalists, dignitaries, and members of the public, all eager to hear the president speak. Hayes, as always, was composed and focused, ready to deliver a message of resilience and determination. As he stepped up to the podium, the room fell silent, and all eyes were on him.

"Ladies and gentlemen," he began, his voice steady and authoritative, "we have faced unprecedented challenges in recent months. The attacks on our infrastructure, the infiltration of our institutions, and the disinformation campaigns have tested our resolve. But we have stood strong. We have worked together, both domestically and with our international allies, to dismantle the network of The Shadow Council. Today, I want to assure you that we will continue this fight until we have rooted out every last trace of corruption and conspiracy."

The audience erupted in applause, a sign of their support and confidence in his leadership. Hayes continued, speaking about the steps being taken to secure the nation's infrastructure, strengthen cybersecurity, and restore public trust. His words were a beacon of hope in a time of uncertainty.

But as he spoke, a shadow moved through the crowd. A figure, dressed inconspicuously, edged closer to the stage. The Secret Service agents, always alert, noticed the movement and began to close in, but they were a fraction of a second too late.

A sharp crack echoed through the room as a gunshot rang out. Chaos erupted, and people screamed and ducked for cover. Hayes felt a searing pain in his shoulder and stumbled backward, the force of the bullet knocking him off balance. The Secret Service agents reacted instantly, surrounding the president and shielding him from further harm.

"Get him out of here!" one of the agents shouted, and they quickly hustled Hayes off the stage and into a waiting vehicle. The motorcade sped away, sirens blaring, as the president was rushed to a secure location.

The nation watched in horror as news of the assassination attempt spread. The attack on President Hayes was a shocking escalation, a clear sign that The Shadow Council was willing to go to any lengths to protect their interests. The media coverage was relentless, and the airwaves were filled with speculation and fear.

At the secure location, Hayes was examined by medical personnel. The bullet had passed cleanly through his shoulder, missing any vital organs, but the wound was painful and would take time to heal. Despite the injury, Hayes remained focused and determined.

"How bad is it?" he asked, gritting his teeth against the pain.

"You were lucky, Mr. President," the doctor replied. "The bullet missed anything critical. You'll need rest and some physical therapy, but you'll make a full recovery."

Hayes nodded, his mind already turning to the implications of the attack. "We need to address the nation. They need to know that I'm okay and that we're still in control."

Olivia Barnes, who had been coordinating the response, stepped forward. "We'll set up a secure broadcast. But we also need to focus on finding out who was behind this. The attack was well-coordinated—this wasn't a lone wolf."

General Marcus Lee, who had arrived with a security detail, added, "Our intelligence teams are already on it. We'll find the shooter and trace this back to whoever orchestrated it."

As the team worked to gather information, Hayes prepared to address the nation from the secure location. The broadcast was set up quickly, and the president appeared on screen, his shoulder bandaged but his demeanor unwavering.

"My fellow Americans," he began, "today, an attempt was made on my life. I want to assure you that I am safe and that we are taking every measure to ensure the security of our nation. This attack is a stark reminder of the threats we face, but it will not deter us. We will continue our fight against The Shadow Council and any other forces that seek to undermine our democracy. Together, we will prevail."

The broadcast had the desired effect, calming public fears and rallying support for the president. But behind the scenes, the administration was in overdrive, working to uncover the full scope of the conspiracy.

The Secret Service and FBI launched an intense investigation to identify the shooter and their connections. They scoured surveillance footage, interviewed witnesses, and analyzed forensic evidence. The initial findings revealed that the shooter had been part of a larger network, with connections to known operatives of The Shadow Council.

As the investigation progressed, more details emerged. The shooter had been a former military contractor with ties to several covert operations. He had been recruited by The Shadow Council for his skills and had been provided with detailed plans and resources to carry out the assassination attempt.

Olivia Barnes and General Lee coordinated closely with the intelligence community, working to piece together the network that had orchestrated the attack. They uncovered a series of encrypted communications that revealed the involvement of high-ranking operatives within The Shadow Council, including some who had previously eluded detection.

The breakthrough came when they identified a key figure coordinating the operation—a shadowy operative known only by the codename "Viper." Viper had been responsible for planning and executing the attack, using a network of operatives and resources to ensure its success. The intelligence teams worked tirelessly to track Viper's movements and uncover his true identity.

Meanwhile, President Hayes continued to lead with determination and resolve. Despite his injury, he remained actively involved in the investigation and the administration's efforts to combat The Shadow Council. He held regular meetings with his advisors, reviewed intelligence reports, and made strategic decisions to protect the nation.

One evening, as Hayes sat in the Oval Office with Olivia and General Lee, Rachel Wu entered with a look of urgency.

"We've made a breakthrough," Rachel said, handing Hayes a report. "We've identified Viper. His real name is Anton Kovalenko, a former Russian intelligence officer who defected and has been working as a mercenary for hire. He's been involved in several high-profile operations, and his connections run deep."

Hayes studied the report, his mind racing with the implications. "Where is he now?"

"We've tracked him to a safe house in Eastern Europe," Rachel replied. "We're coordinating with our international partners to apprehend him. This could be our chance to dismantle a significant part of The Shadow Council's network."

The plan to capture Kovalenko was meticulously coordinated. The task force, composed of elite operatives from the U.S. and its international allies, prepared for the operation with precision. They knew that capturing Kovalenko would not only provide valuable intelligence but also deal a significant blow to The Shadow Council.

The raid on the safe house was executed with military precision. The operatives moved in swiftly, securing the perimeter and breaching the building. Inside, they found Kovalenko and several of his associates, who were taken into custody without incident.

The captured operatives were transported to a secure facility for interrogation. The intelligence gathered from Kovalenko was invaluable, revealing critical details about The Shadow Council's operations, funding, and future plans. Kovalenko, under intense pressure, provided information that led to the identification of other high-ranking operatives and the locations of key facilities.

With this new intelligence, the administration launched a series of coordinated operations to dismantle The Shadow Council's network. The combined efforts of the intelligence community, military, and law enforcement agencies resulted in significant successes, disrupting the network's activities and apprehending key figures.

As the operations continued, public confidence in the administration began to recover. The transparency and determination shown by President Hayes and his team reassured the nation that they were taking decisive action to protect the country and restore order.

In a televised address, Hayes updated the nation on the progress made in dismantling The Shadow Council's network.

"My fellow Americans," he began, "thanks to the tireless efforts of our intelligence and security teams, we have made significant progress in our fight against The Shadow Council. We have captured key operatives and disrupted their operations. But our work is not done. We will continue to pursue justice and ensure the safety of our nation. Together, we will overcome this threat and emerge stronger."

The response from the public was overwhelmingly positive, and support for the president surged. The attempted assassination, rather than weakening his administration, had galvanized the nation and demonstrated the resilience and resolve of its leadership.

As the administration continued its efforts to dismantle The Shadow Council's network, they remained vigilant and proactive. The threat was far from eliminated, but with each success, they moved closer to their goal.

One evening, as Hayes reflected on the progress they had made, Olivia entered his office with a look of determination.

"Mr. President, we've identified another key facility used by The Shadow Council," she said, handing him a report. "This facility is believed to be a central hub for their cyber operations. Taking it down could significantly weaken their capabilities."

Hayes reviewed the report, his resolve unwavering. "Let's move forward with the operation. We need to keep the pressure on them and disrupt their activities at every turn."

The operation to take down the cyber facility was planned with the same precision and coordination as the previous raids. The task force, composed of cyber operatives and field agents, prepared to strike swiftly and decisively.

The raid was executed flawlessly. The operatives breached the facility, securing critical servers and equipment and apprehending the personnel inside. The intelligence gathered from the operation provided valuable insights into The Shadow Council's cyber capabilities and plans.

With each success, the administration's efforts to combat The Shadow Council gained momentum. The public's confidence continued to grow, and the nation's resilience was evident.

As President Hayes addressed the nation once again, his tone was one of determination and hope.

"My fellow Americans, our fight against The Shadow Council continues, and we are making significant progress. Our efforts to dismantle their network and protect our nation are yielding results. We remain vigilant and committed to justice. Together, we will prevail."

The administration's efforts were recognized and celebrated, and President Hayes emerged as a symbol of integrity and resilience. The fight against The Shadow Council had tested their resolve, but it had also strengthened their commitment to justice and the values that defined their nation.

Throughout this tumultuous period, the support and loyalty of the task force were crucial. Olivia Barnes continued to coordinate the operation with unwavering dedication, and General Lee provided invaluable strategic guidance. Together, they navigated the complexities of the situation and worked tirelessly to protect the administration and the nation.

One evening, as President Hayes sat in the Oval Office reflecting on the progress they had made, Olivia entered with a determined look on her face.

"Mr. President, we've identified another key operative within The Shadow Council," she said, handing him a report. "This operative has been coordinating the disinformation campaign and is responsible for many of the cyberattacks we've faced."

Hayes felt a surge of determination. "We need to take them down. What's the plan?"

Olivia outlined the operation, which involved a coordinated effort between cyber operatives and field agents. Rachel Wu would lead the cyber aspect, using advanced techniques to breach the operative's digital defenses and gather critical intelligence. John Carter's team would handle the physical apprehension, conducting a raid to capture the operative and secure any evidence.

The operation was meticulously planned and executed. Rachel's team launched a cyberattack to disrupt the operative's communications and coordination, while John's team moved in to apprehend the target. The raid was a success, resulting in the capture of the operative and the seizure of critical evidence.

The captured operative provided valuable intelligence, revealing more about The Shadow Council's operations and plans. The administration used this intelligence to launch further operations, disrupting key activities and weakening the network's hold.

Despite the successes, the fight was far from over. The Shadow Council continued to adapt and evolve, using their resources and influence to mount new attacks and spread disinformation. The administration had to remain vigilant and proactive, constantly adjusting their strategies to stay ahead of the enemy.

As the weeks passed, the team's efforts began to yield significant results. The public started to see the administration's determination and resilience, and confidence slowly began to return. The stock market stabilized, and financial institutions resumed normal operations. Power grids were secured, and communication networks were restored.

President Hayes addressed the nation once again, his tone resolute and hopeful. "My fellow Americans, we have faced an unprecedented challenge, but we have stood strong. Our efforts to dismantle The Shadow Council's network are yielding results, and we are restoring stability and security. We will continue to fight for the integrity of our nation and the trust of our people. Together, we will emerge from this stronger and more united."

The administration's efforts were recognized and celebrated, and President Hayes emerged as a symbol of integrity and resilience. The fight against The Shadow Council had tested their resolve, but it had also strengthened their commitment to justice and the values that defined their nation.

As the administration continued its efforts to protect the nation and restore public trust, President Hayes knew that the journey was far from over. The fight against corruption and betrayal would be ongoing, but with the support of a dedicated team and the determination to see it through, they would prevail.

The shadows of The Shadow Council had been exposed, and the path ahead was clear. Together, they had faced the darkness and emerged victorious, and the future was bright with the promise of justice and integrity.

The presidency was a heavy burden, but it was one that Hayes bore with honor and a deep sense of responsibility. The challenges had been immense, but they had demonstrated their commitment to justice and the values that defined their nation. The journey was far from over, but with each step, they moved closer to building a brighter and more secure future.

The betrayal had been unveiled, and the fight against corruption continued. But with the strength and resolve of President Hayes and his team, the nation was in capable hands. The future was theirs to shape, and they were ready to face it with unwavering determination and a steadfast commitment to justice.

Chapter 12: The Race Against Time

The chill of a Washington winter morning seeped through the walls of the White House, but President Daniel Hayes barely felt it. The atmosphere inside was electric with urgency. The Shadow Council, though significantly weakened by the administration's relentless efforts, was far from defeated. Intelligence reports indicated that the threat was escalating, and Hayes knew that his team was racing against time to expose and stop their enemies.

It was early, but Hayes was already in the Situation Room, surrounded by his closest advisors. Olivia Barnes, his chief of staff, was seated beside him, her face etched with concentration. General Marcus Lee stood at the head of the table, his military bearing exuding a sense of readiness and determination. Rachel Wu, their cybersecurity expert, was busy setting up the latest intelligence reports on the large screens that dominated the room.

Hayes opened the meeting with a sense of gravity. "We have reliable intelligence indicating that The Shadow Council is planning a major terrorist attack aimed at destabilizing the government. This is a race against time, and we need to move swiftly and decisively to stop them."

Rachel Wu began her presentation, displaying a series of intercepted communications and encrypted messages. "Our cybersecurity team has uncovered plans for a coordinated attack targeting multiple locations across the capital. The attack is designed to cause maximum chaos and disruption, hitting key government buildings, infrastructure, and public places simultaneously."

General Lee took over, pointing to a map that highlighted the potential targets. "Their primary objective is to create widespread panic and destabilize the government. The intelligence suggests that they have already planted operatives and resources in strategic positions. We need to identify and neutralize these threats immediately."

Olivia Barnes added, "We also need to manage the public response. The threat of a major terrorist attack will undoubtedly cause fear and anxiety. We need to communicate clearly and effectively to maintain public trust and order."

As the team discussed their strategy, Hayes felt a surge of determination. The stakes had never been higher, and the nation was counting on their leadership. The plan required coordination on multiple fronts—cybersecurity, intelligence gathering, military operations, and public communication.

The first step was to enhance their surveillance and intelligence capabilities. Rachel Wu's team worked around the clock, using advanced algorithms and hacking techniques to penetrate The Shadow Council's digital defenses. They monitored communications, traced financial transactions, and analyzed patterns to identify the operatives involved in the planned attack.

Simultaneously, John Carter, the experienced CIA operative, led a team of field agents to track down and apprehend known associates of The Shadow Council. They conducted raids on suspected safe houses, interrogated captured operatives, and followed every lead to uncover the details of the attack.

General Lee coordinated with the Department of Defense and local law enforcement to prepare for potential threats. They increased security at key locations, conducted drills to respond to multiple attack scenarios, and deployed additional resources to protect critical infrastructure.

As the days passed, the tension in the White House grew palpable. The team was making progress, but time was running out. Every new piece of intelligence brought them closer to understanding the full scope of the threat, but it also revealed the complexity and scale of the planned attack.

One evening, as Hayes reviewed the latest reports in the Oval Office, Olivia entered with a look of urgency. "Mr. President, we've uncovered a critical piece of information. The Shadow Council's operatives have already planted explosives at several key locations. We need to act immediately to defuse them and apprehend the operatives involved."

Hayes felt a chill run down his spine. "What's the plan?"

Olivia outlined the operation, which involved a coordinated effort between cybersecurity, intelligence, and military teams. Rachel's team would provide real-time intelligence to identify the locations of the explosives and the operatives. John's field agents would move in to defuse the explosives and apprehend the operatives, while General Lee's forces would secure the perimeter and provide backup.

The operation was launched with precision and urgency. Rachel's team worked tirelessly to pinpoint the locations of the explosives, using their advanced tools to hack into surveillance systems and trace communications. They identified multiple targets, including government buildings, transportation hubs, and public venues.

John Carter and his field agents moved swiftly, conducting raids on the identified locations. They defused the explosives with the help of bomb disposal experts and apprehended several operatives involved in the plot. The raids were executed flawlessly, but the threat was far from over.

As the operation continued, the team uncovered more information about the planned attack. The Shadow Council had not only planted explosives but also planned to use cyberattacks to create further chaos. Their goal was to cripple the government's response and amplify the impact of the physical attacks.

Rachel's team shifted their focus to countering the cyber threats. They identified the digital infrastructure used by The Shadow Council to coordinate the attacks and launched a series of cyber offensives to disrupt their operations. The battle in cyberspace was intense, with both sides using advanced techniques to outmaneuver each other.

Despite the challenges, the administration's efforts began to yield results. The combined operations in the field and in cyberspace disrupted The Shadow Council's plans and significantly weakened their capabilities. The public, initially gripped by fear, started to regain confidence as news of the successful operations spread.

President Hayes addressed the nation in a televised speech, his tone resolute and reassuring. "My fellow Americans, we are facing a coordinated and unprecedented threat, but we are taking decisive action to protect our nation. Our intelligence and security teams have thwarted multiple attacks and apprehended several operatives. We remain vigilant and committed to your safety. Together, we will overcome this challenge and emerge stronger."

The president's address had a calming effect, but the team knew that the fight was far from over. The Shadow Council was a formidable adversary, and they were likely to regroup and launch new attacks. The administration had to remain proactive and adaptive to stay ahead of the threat.

As the days turned into weeks, the team continued their relentless efforts to dismantle The Shadow Council's network. They conducted more raids, gathered critical intelligence, and disrupted operations both in the field and in cyberspace. Each success brought them closer to their goal, but the journey was fraught with challenges.

One particularly challenging operation involved a high-risk raid on a suspected Shadow Council command center. The intelligence indicated that this facility was a central hub for coordinating the planned attacks and housed key operatives and resources. The raid required meticulous planning and coordination, with the involvement of multiple agencies and international partners.

The operation began under the cover of darkness, with teams moving swiftly to secure the perimeter and breach the facility. Inside, they encountered fierce resistance from well-armed operatives. The firefight was intense, but the team's training and determination prevailed. They secured the facility, apprehended the operatives, and seized critical intelligence.

The intelligence gathered from the raid provided invaluable insights into The Shadow Council's operations and plans. It revealed the identities of several high-ranking operatives, their communication networks, and their financial resources. The administration used this information to launch further operations, disrupting key activities and weakening the network's hold.

Despite the successes, the team remained on high alert. The threat of a major terrorist attack was ever-present, and they knew that The Shadow Council would stop at nothing to achieve their goals. The administration continued to work tirelessly, coordinating efforts across multiple fronts to protect the nation and its people.

As the weeks passed, the public began to see the administration's determination and resilience. Confidence slowly began to return, and the nation rallied behind President Hayes and his team. The fight against The Shadow Council had tested their resolve, but it had also strengthened their commitment to justice and the values that defined their nation.

One evening, as Hayes sat in the Oval Office reflecting on the progress they had made, Olivia entered with a determined look on her face.

"Mr. President, we've identified another key operative within The Shadow Council," she said, handing him a report. "This operative has been coordinating the disinformation campaign and is responsible for many of the cyberattacks we've faced."

Hayes felt a surge of determination. "We need to take them down. What's the plan?"

Olivia outlined the operation, which involved a coordinated effort between cyber operatives and field agents. Rachel Wu would lead the cyber aspect, using advanced techniques to breach the operative's digital defenses and gather critical intelligence. John Carter's team would handle the physical apprehension, conducting a raid to capture the operative and secure any evidence.

The operation was meticulously planned and executed. Rachel's team launched a cyberattack to disrupt the operative's communications and coordination, while John's team moved in to apprehend the target. The raid was a success, resulting in the capture of the operative and the seizure of critical evidence.

The captured operative provided valuable intelligence, revealing more about The Shadow Council's operations and plans. The administration used this intelligence to launch further operations, disrupting key activities and weakening the network's hold.

Despite the successes, the fight was far from over. The Shadow Council continued to adapt and evolve, using their resources and influence to mount new attacks and spread disinformation. The administration had to remain vigilant and proactive, constantly adjusting their strategies to stay ahead of the enemy.

As the weeks passed, the team's efforts began to yield significant results. The public started to see the administration's determination and resilience, and confidence slowly began to return. The stock market stabilized, and financial institutions resumed normal operations. Power grids were secured, and communication networks were restored.

President Hayes addressed the nation once again, his tone resolute and hopeful. "My fellow Americans, we have faced an unprecedented challenge, but we have stood strong. Our efforts to dismantle The Shadow Council's network are yielding results, and we are restoring stability and security. We will continue to fight for the integrity of our nation and the trust of our people. Together, we will emerge from this stronger and more united."

The administration's efforts were recognized and celebrated, and President Hayes emerged as a symbol of integrity and resilience. The fight against The Shadow Council had tested their resolve, but it had also strengthened their commitment to justice and the values that defined their nation.

Throughout this tumultuous period, the support and loyalty of the task force were crucial. Olivia Barnes continued to coordinate the operation with unwavering dedication, and General Lee provided invaluable strategic guidance. Together, they navigated the complexities of the situation and worked tirelessly to protect the administration and the nation.

One evening, as President Hayes sat in the Oval Office reflecting on the progress they had made, Olivia entered with a determined look on her face.

"Mr. President, we've identified another key operative within The Shadow Council," she said, handing him a report. "This operative has been coordinating the disinformation campaign and is responsible for many of the cyberattacks we've faced."

Hayes felt a surge of determination. "We need to take them down. What's the plan?"

Olivia outlined the operation, which involved a coordinated effort between cyber operatives and field agents. Rachel Wu would lead the cyber aspect, using advanced techniques to breach the operative's digital defenses and gather critical intelligence. John Carter's team would handle the physical apprehension, conducting a raid to capture the operative and secure any evidence.

The operation was meticulously planned and executed. Rachel's team launched a cyberattack to disrupt the operative's communications and coordination, while John's team moved in to apprehend the target. The raid was a success, resulting in the capture of the operative and the seizure of critical evidence.

The captured operative provided valuable intelligence, revealing more about The Shadow Council's operations and plans. The administration used this intelligence to launch further operations, disrupting key activities and weakening the network's hold.

Despite the successes, the fight was far from over. The Shadow Council continued to adapt and evolve, using their resources and influence to mount new attacks and spread disinformation. The administration had to remain vigilant and proactive, constantly adjusting their strategies to stay ahead of the enemy.

As the weeks passed, the team's efforts began to yield significant results. The public started to see the administration's determination and resilience, and confidence slowly began to return. The stock market stabilized, and financial institutions resumed normal operations. Power grids were secured, and communication networks were restored.

President Hayes addressed the nation once again, his tone resolute and hopeful. "My fellow Americans, we have faced an unprecedented challenge, but we have stood strong. Our efforts to dismantle The Shadow Council's network are yielding results, and we are restoring stability and security. We will continue to fight for the integrity of our nation and the trust of our people. Together, we will emerge from this stronger and more united."

The administration's efforts were recognized and celebrated, and President Hayes emerged as a symbol of integrity and resilience. The fight against The Shadow Council had tested their resolve, but it had also strengthened their commitment to justice and the values that defined their nation.

As the administration continued its efforts to protect the nation and restore public trust, President Hayes knew that the journey was far from over. The fight against corruption and betrayal would be ongoing, but with the support of a dedicated team and the determination to see it through, they would prevail.

The shadows of The Shadow Council had been exposed, and the path ahead was clear. Together, they had faced the darkness and emerged victorious, and the future was bright with the promise of justice and integrity.

The presidency was a heavy burden, but it was one that Hayes bore with honor and a deep sense of responsibility. The challenges had been immense, but they had demonstrated their commitment to justice and the values that defined their nation. The journey was far from over, but with each step, they moved closer to building a brighter and more secure future.

The betrayal had been unveiled, and the fight against corruption continued. But with the strength and resolve of President Hayes and his team, the nation was in capable hands. The future was theirs to shape, and they were ready to face it with unwavering determination and a steadfast commitment to justice.

As the administration continued its efforts to dismantle The Shadow Council's network, they remained vigilant and proactive. The enemy was cunning and resilient, but the administration's determination and resolve were unwavering.

One evening, as President Hayes sat in the Oval Office reflecting on the progress they had made, Olivia entered with a determined look on her face.

"Mr. President, we've identified another key operative within The Shadow Council," she said, handing him a report. "This operative has been coordinating the disinformation campaign and is responsible for many of the cyberattacks we've faced."

Hayes felt a surge of determination. "We need to take them down. What's the plan?"

Olivia outlined the operation, which involved a coordinated effort between cyber operatives and field agents. Rachel Wu would lead the cyber aspect, using advanced techniques to breach the operative's digital defenses and gather critical intelligence. John Carter's team would handle the physical apprehension, conducting a raid to capture the operative and secure any evidence.

The operation was meticulously planned and executed. Rachel's team launched a cyberattack to disrupt the operative's communications and coordination, while John's team moved in to apprehend the target. The raid was a success, resulting in the capture of the operative and the seizure of critical evidence.

The captured operative provided valuable intelligence, revealing more about The Shadow Council's operations and plans. The administration used this intelligence to launch further operations, disrupting key activities and weakening the network's hold.

Despite the successes, the fight was far from over. The Shadow Council continued to adapt and evolve, using their resources and influence to mount new attacks and spread disinformation. The administration had to remain vigilant and proactive, constantly adjusting their strategies to stay ahead of the enemy.

As the weeks passed, the team's efforts began to yield significant results. The public started to see the administration's determination and resilience, and confidence slowly began to return. The stock market stabilized, and financial institutions resumed normal operations. Power grids were secured, and communication networks were restored.

President Hayes addressed the nation once again, his tone resolute and hopeful. "My fellow Americans, we have faced an unprecedented challenge, but we have stood strong. Our efforts to dismantle The Shadow Council's network are yielding results, and we are restoring stability and security. We will continue to fight for the integrity of our nation and the trust of our people. Together, we will emerge from this stronger and more united."

The administration's efforts were recognized and celebrated, and President Hayes emerged as a symbol of integrity and resilience. The fight against The Shadow Council had tested their resolve, but it had also strengthened their commitment to justice and the values that defined their nation.

As the administration continued its efforts to protect the nation and restore public trust, President Hayes knew that the journey was far from over. The fight against corruption and betrayal would be ongoing, but with the support of a dedicated team and the determination to see it through, they would prevail.

The shadows of The Shadow Council had been exposed, and the path ahead was clear. Together, they had faced the darkness and emerged victorious, and the future was bright with the promise of justice and integrity.

The presidency was a heavy burden, but it was one that Hayes bore with honor and a deep sense of responsibility. The challenges had been immense, but they had demonstrated their commitment to justice and the values that defined their nation. The journey was far from over, but with each step, they moved closer to building a brighter and more secure future.

The betrayal had been unveiled, and the fight against corruption continued. But with the strength and resolve of President Hayes and his team, the nation was in capable hands. The future was theirs to shape, and they were ready to face it with unwavering determination and a steadfast commitment to justice.

Chapter 13: The Final Confrontation

The icy wind howled through the streets of Washington, D.C., but President Daniel Hayes barely noticed as he stood in the Situation Room. The air inside was charged with anticipation and determination. They were on the cusp of the final confrontation with The Shadow Council, a showdown that would determine the future of the nation.

For months, the administration had fought tirelessly against the shadowy network that had infiltrated the highest levels of government and sought to destabilize the nation. Their efforts had yielded significant victories, but The Shadow Council remained a potent threat. Now, with critical intelligence in hand, Hayes, his chief of staff Olivia Barnes, and General Marcus Lee were preparing for a daring mission to strike at the heart of The Shadow Council's operations.

Olivia Barnes stood next to Hayes, her face set in a mask of determination. General Lee, with his military precision, outlined the details of the operation. On the large screen in front of them was a map displaying the location of The Shadow Council's primary command center—a fortified compound deep in the mountains of Eastern Europe. This facility was the nerve center of their operations, housing their top leaders and critical resources.

"We've identified the location of their command center," General Lee began, pointing to the map. "It's heavily fortified and protected by advanced security systems. Our intelligence indicates that their top leaders are currently there, coordinating their operations. This is our chance to strike a decisive blow and dismantle their network once and for all."

Olivia added, "This mission will be high-risk. We'll need to infiltrate the compound, neutralize the security systems, and apprehend their leaders. We've assembled a team of our best operatives, including cybersecurity experts, intelligence officers, and special forces. This is an all-hands-on-deck operation."

Hayes nodded, his mind racing with the implications. "What's our plan for entry and extraction?"

General Lee outlined the strategy. "We'll deploy in two phases. The first phase involves a cyber offensive led by Rachel Wu and her team. They'll disable the compound's security systems and communications. The second phase involves a ground assault led by John Carter and our special forces. They'll infiltrate the compound, secure the perimeter, and apprehend the targets."

The president felt a surge of determination. "Let's move forward. We need to end this once and for all."

As the team prepared for the mission, the atmosphere was tense but resolute. Each member knew the stakes and was ready to face the challenge head-on. They worked tirelessly, coordinating every detail and ensuring that all contingencies were covered.

The night of the operation was cold and clear. The team assembled at a secure airbase, where they boarded a fleet of helicopters and transport planes. The aircraft would take them to a staging area near the target location, from where they would launch the assault.

Rachel Wu and her cybersecurity team worked from a mobile command center, equipped with the latest technology to penetrate and disable The Shadow Council's security systems. They monitored the compound's communications and identified vulnerabilities in their defenses.

As the aircraft flew through the night, Hayes, Olivia, and General Lee reviewed the final details of the mission. Each of them was keenly aware of the risks, but their resolve was unshakable. They knew that this was their best chance to dismantle The Shadow Council and secure the future of the nation.

The aircraft landed at the staging area, a remote location hidden from prying eyes. The team quickly disembarked and prepared for the assault. Rachel and her team set up their equipment, ready to launch the cyber offensive. John Carter and the special forces operatives checked their gear and reviewed their roles.

Hayes addressed the team, his voice steady and resolute. "This is it. We've fought long and hard to get to this point. The Shadow Council has caused untold damage, but tonight, we have the opportunity to end their reign. Stay focused, stay sharp, and let's get this done."

The team moved out, blending into the night as they approached the compound. Rachel and her team launched the cyber offensive, hacking into the compound's security systems and disabling their communications. The screens in the command center lit up with activity as Rachel's team executed their plan with precision.

"We're in," Rachel announced. "Their security systems are down, and their communications are offline. You're clear to move in."

John Carter and the special forces operatives moved swiftly, breaching the perimeter and entering the compound. They encountered resistance from armed guards, but their training and coordination allowed them to neutralize the threats quickly and efficiently.

As they moved deeper into the compound, the tension mounted. The corridors were dimly lit, and the air was thick with anticipation. They reached the central control room, where they found several of The Shadow Council's leaders coordinating their operations.

"Hands up! Don't move!" John commanded, his voice echoing through the room.

The leaders complied, their faces a mixture of shock and defiance. The operatives quickly secured the room, apprehending the targets and gathering critical intelligence. The mission was progressing smoothly, but they knew that the hardest part was yet to come.

As they secured the compound, an unexpected development occurred. A group of operatives, dressed in tactical gear, emerged from a hidden passage. They were not part of The Shadow Council's forces, and their presence took everyone by surprise.

"Stand down! We're here to help," one of the operatives announced, raising his hands in a gesture of peace.

John Carter and his team hesitated, their weapons trained on the newcomers. "Identify yourselves," John demanded.

The leader of the new group stepped forward, removing his helmet. "I'm Alexei Petrov, former Russian intelligence. We've been tracking The Shadow Council as well, and we have a common enemy. We're here to assist you in taking them down."

The revelation of unexpected allies added a new layer of complexity to the mission. Hayes, monitoring the situation from the mobile command center, was briefed on the development.

"Proceed with caution," Hayes instructed. "If they're genuine, they could be valuable allies. But trust must be earned."

The combined forces moved through the compound, securing additional areas and gathering more intelligence. The presence of the former Russian operatives provided valuable insights into The Shadow Council's operations and connections.

As they reached the innermost sanctum of the compound, they encountered the heart of The Shadow Council's leadership. The room was filled with high-ranking operatives, including the elusive figure known as Viper. The atmosphere was tense, and a showdown was imminent.

"Your reign of terror ends here," Hayes declared, his voice echoing through the room. "Surrender now, and you will face justice."

Viper, a tall and imposing figure, stepped forward. His eyes were cold and calculating. "You're too late, President Hayes. Our network is vast, and our reach is beyond your comprehension. Even if you take us down here, others will rise in our place."

Hayes remained resolute. "We will not stop until every last one of you is brought to justice. Your time is up."

A tense standoff ensued, with both sides ready for a final confrontation. The operatives, both American and Russian, stood side by side, their weapons trained on The Shadow Council's leaders.

The silence was broken by the sound of a gunshot. One of The Shadow Council's operatives, attempting to make a last-ditch effort to escape, had fired his weapon. The room erupted into chaos as gunfire was exchanged.

The firefight was intense, but the training and coordination of Hayes's team prevailed. Within minutes, the room was secured, and The Shadow Council's leaders were apprehended. Viper, realizing that his defeat was imminent, made a final desperate move.

"You may have won this battle, but the war is far from over," Viper hissed, reaching for a concealed weapon.

John Carter reacted swiftly, disarming Viper and securing him. "Not today," John said, his voice steady.

The mission was a resounding success. The compound was secured, The Shadow Council's leaders were captured, and critical intelligence was gathered. The team, though exhausted, felt a sense of triumph and relief.

As they prepared to extract the captives and return to the staging area, Hayes addressed his team. "This is a significant victory, but our work is not done. We need to use the intelligence we've gathered to dismantle the remaining elements of The Shadow Council and ensure that they cannot rise again."

The extraction was executed smoothly, and the team returned to the staging area with their captives and intelligence. The former Russian operatives, now trusted allies, provided additional insights and resources to aid in the ongoing efforts.

Back in Washington, the nation watched with bated breath as news of the mission spread. The public's confidence in the administration was bolstered by the decisive action and the successful outcome of the operation.

President Hayes addressed the nation once again, his tone one of resolve and hope. "My fellow Americans, today we achieved a significant victory in our fight against The Shadow Council. We have captured their leaders and secured critical intelligence to dismantle their network. This is a testament to the strength and resilience of our nation. We will continue to fight for justice and ensure the safety and security of our people. Together, we will prevail."

The administration's efforts were recognized and celebrated, and President Hayes emerged as a symbol of integrity and resilience. The fight against The Shadow Council had tested their resolve, but it had also strengthened their commitment to justice and the values that defined their nation.

Throughout this tumultuous period, the support and loyalty of the task force were crucial. Olivia Barnes continued to coordinate the operation with unwavering dedication, and General Lee provided invaluable strategic guidance. Together, they navigated the complexities of the situation and worked tirelessly to protect the administration and the nation.

One evening, as President Hayes sat in the Oval Office reflecting on the progress they had made, Olivia entered with a determined look on her face.

"Mr. President, we've identified another key operative within The Shadow Council," she said, handing him a report. "This operative has been coordinating the disinformation campaign and is responsible for many of the cyberattacks we've faced."

Hayes felt a surge of determination. "We need to take them down. What's the plan?"

Olivia outlined the operation, which involved a coordinated effort between cyber operatives and field agents. Rachel Wu would lead the cyber aspect, using advanced techniques to breach the operative's digital defenses and gather critical intelligence. John Carter's team would handle the physical apprehension, conducting a raid to capture the operative and secure any evidence.

The operation was meticulously planned and executed. Rachel's team launched a cyberattack to disrupt the operative's communications and coordination, while John's team moved in to apprehend the target. The raid was a success, resulting in the capture of the operative and the seizure of critical evidence.

The captured operative provided valuable intelligence, revealing more about The Shadow Council's operations and plans. The administration used this intelligence to launch further operations, disrupting key activities and weakening the network's hold.

Despite the successes, the fight was far from over. The Shadow Council continued to adapt and evolve, using their resources and influence to mount new attacks and spread disinformation. The administration had to remain vigilant and proactive, constantly adjusting their strategies to stay ahead of the enemy.

As the weeks passed, the team's efforts began to yield significant results. The public started to see the administration's determination and resilience, and confidence slowly began to return. The stock market stabilized, and financial institutions resumed normal operations. Power grids were secured, and communication networks were restored.

President Hayes addressed the nation once again, his tone resolute and hopeful. "My fellow Americans, we have faced an unprecedented challenge, but we have stood strong. Our efforts to dismantle The Shadow Council's network are yielding results, and we are restoring stability and security. We will continue to fight for the integrity of our nation and the trust of our people. Together, we will emerge from this stronger and more united."

The administration's efforts were recognized and celebrated, and President Hayes emerged as a symbol of integrity and resilience. The fight against The Shadow Council had tested their resolve, but it had also strengthened their commitment to justice and the values that defined their nation.

As the administration continued its efforts to protect the nation and restore public trust, President Hayes knew that the journey was far from over. The fight against corruption and betrayal would be ongoing, but with the support of a dedicated team and the determination to see it through, they would prevail.

The shadows of The Shadow Council had been exposed, and the path ahead was clear. Together, they had faced the darkness and emerged victorious, and the future was bright with the promise of justice and integrity.

The presidency was a heavy burden, but it was one that Hayes bore with honor and a deep sense of responsibility. The challenges had been immense, but they had demonstrated their commitment to justice and the values that defined their nation. The journey was far from over, but with each step, they moved closer to building a brighter and more secure future.

The betrayal had been unveiled, and the fight against corruption continued. But with the strength and resolve of President Hayes and his team, the nation was in capable hands. The future was theirs to shape, and they were ready to face it with unwavering determination and a steadfast commitment to justice.

Chapter 14: The Aftermath

The dawn broke over Washington, D.C., casting a soft light on the city that had been the epicenter of a seismic struggle. President Daniel Hayes stood at the window of the Oval Office, looking out at the capital, his heart heavy with the knowledge of the sacrifices made in the battle against The Shadow Council. The immediate threat had been neutralized, but the cost had been high. Many lives had been lost, and the nation was grappling with the aftermath of the intense conflict.

Inside the White House, the atmosphere was one of somber reflection and quiet determination. The battle had taken its toll on everyone involved, from the highest levels of government to the operatives on the ground. The victory was bittersweet, marked by the profound loss of those who had given their lives to protect the nation.

President Hayes turned from the window as Olivia Barnes, his chief of staff, entered the room. Her face was etched with fatigue and sorrow, but also with a sense of purpose. "Mr. President, the final casualty reports are in," she said softly, handing him a file.

Hayes took the file, his heart heavy as he read through the names and numbers. Each life lost was a painful reminder of the cost of their fight against corruption and tyranny. "How are we holding up, Olivia?" he asked, his voice tinged with the weight of the past months.

Olivia sighed. "It's been incredibly hard, sir. The team is exhausted, and morale is low. But they're also proud of what we've accomplished. We've dealt a significant blow to The Shadow Council, and the nation is beginning to heal."

Hayes nodded, his mind racing with thoughts of the sacrifices made and the challenges that lay ahead. "We need to ensure that their sacrifices were not in vain. We have to rebuild, restore trust, and continue to root out any remnants of corruption."

As they spoke, General Marcus Lee entered the room, his expression grim but resolute. "Mr. President, we've secured the compound and gathered all the intelligence we could find. Our teams are analyzing the data, but it's clear that The Shadow Council's network was vast and deeply entrenched."

Hayes felt a surge of determination. "We need to stay vigilant. Even though we've taken down their leaders, there may still be operatives out there trying to regroup. We can't let our guard down."

General Lee agreed. "We're conducting follow-up operations to ensure that we dismantle any remaining cells. Our intelligence teams are working around the clock to track down any leads."

The immediate threat had been neutralized, but the battle against corruption was far from over. Hayes knew that the challenges of leadership extended beyond the battlefield. The nation needed healing, and the government needed to restore the public's trust.

Later that day, Hayes convened a meeting with his top advisors to discuss the next steps. The room was filled with a mix of relief and resolve, as they prepared to address the nation and begin the process of rebuilding.

"Thank you all for being here," Hayes began, his voice steady. "We've achieved a significant victory, but we've also paid a heavy price. Our first priority must be to honor those who have fallen and support their families. We also need to focus on rebuilding our institutions and restoring public trust."

Olivia nodded. "We'll organize a national memorial service to honor the fallen. It's important that we recognize their sacrifices and provide support to their families."

Hayes agreed. "We also need to communicate clearly with the public about what we've accomplished and the steps we're taking to ensure their safety. Transparency will be key in rebuilding trust."

Rachel Wu, the cybersecurity expert, spoke up. "We've gathered a wealth of intelligence from the compound. It's going to take time to analyze everything, but we're already identifying connections and networks that we can dismantle. This will be an ongoing effort."

John Carter, the CIA operative, added, "We've also apprehended several key operatives who are providing valuable information. We're interrogating them and following up on every lead. It's clear that The Shadow Council's influence was far-reaching, but we're making progress."

As the meeting continued, the team discussed the steps needed to rebuild and restore the nation's institutions. They outlined plans for strengthening cybersecurity, enhancing intelligence operations, and improving coordination between agencies. The focus was on ensuring that the nation was better prepared to prevent and respond to future threats.

That evening, President Hayes addressed the nation in a televised speech. His face was solemn, but his voice carried a message of hope and resilience.

"My fellow Americans," he began, "we have faced an unprecedented challenge, and we have emerged stronger. The Shadow Council sought to undermine our democracy and destabilize our nation, but we stood firm. We fought back, and we prevailed. However, this victory has come at a great cost. Many brave men and women have given their lives to protect our freedoms and ensure our safety. We honor their sacrifice, and we vow to continue their fight."

Hayes paused, his eyes reflecting the weight of his words. "We are committed to rebuilding and restoring our nation. We will strengthen our institutions, enhance our security, and ensure that those who seek to harm us are brought to justice. We will also provide support to the families of those who have fallen and honor their memory."

The president's address struck a chord with the nation. The public, though grieving the losses, found solace in the administration's determination and transparency. The sense of unity and resolve that had been forged in the crucible of conflict began to permeate the national consciousness.

In the weeks that followed, the administration focused on implementing their plans for rebuilding and strengthening the nation. They conducted a thorough review of security protocols, identified areas for improvement, and implemented new measures to prevent future threats.

The national memorial service was a poignant and solemn event. Held on the steps of the Capitol, it was attended by government officials, military personnel, and families of the fallen. President Hayes delivered a heartfelt eulogy, honoring the bravery and sacrifice of those who had given their lives in the fight against The Shadow Council.

"We gather here today to honor the heroes who have fallen in the defense of our nation," Hayes began, his voice resonating with emotion. "Their courage and sacrifice have ensured our freedom and protected our democracy. We owe them a debt of gratitude that can never be repaid, but we can honor their memory by continuing their fight and upholding the values they died to protect."

As the nation mourned and honored the fallen, the administration continued its relentless pursuit of any remaining elements of The Shadow Council. The intelligence gathered from the compound provided a roadmap for dismantling the network's infrastructure and identifying hidden operatives.

One evening, as Hayes sat in the Oval Office reviewing the latest intelligence reports, Olivia entered with a look of determination. "Mr. President, we've identified several high-ranking operatives who are still at large. Our teams are preparing to launch coordinated operations to apprehend them."

Hayes felt a renewed sense of purpose. "Let's make sure we get them. We can't allow any remnants of The Shadow Council to regroup or continue their activities."

The operations were meticulously planned and executed, resulting in the capture of several key figures and the disruption of remaining cells. The administration's efforts were yielding significant results, but the pervasive nature of corruption remained a constant challenge.

As the weeks turned into months, the nation slowly began to heal. The administration's focus on transparency, accountability, and rebuilding trust resonated with the public. The sense of unity and resilience that had been forged in the face of adversity became a source of strength.

President Hayes reflected on the challenges of leadership and the pervasive nature of corruption. The battle against The Shadow Council had revealed the depth and complexity of the threats facing the nation. It had also underscored the importance of vigilance, integrity, and unwavering commitment to justice.

In a private conversation with Olivia, Hayes shared his thoughts. "This fight has shown us the lengths to which those who seek power will go to achieve their goals. Corruption is a cancer that can infiltrate every level of society. Our task is not just to root it out, but to build systems and institutions that are resilient and transparent."

Olivia nodded, her expression thoughtful. "It's a long and difficult journey, but we've made significant progress. The public's trust is slowly being restored, and our efforts are making a difference. We need to keep pushing forward and remain vigilant."

Hayes agreed. "We've faced immense challenges, but we've also demonstrated the strength and resilience of our nation. We've shown that we can stand up to corruption and protect our democracy. The road ahead will be difficult, but we're prepared to face it."

The administration continued its efforts to strengthen the nation's institutions and ensure accountability. They implemented new policies and reforms aimed at preventing corruption, enhancing cybersecurity, and improving coordination between agencies. The focus was on creating a government that was transparent, accountable, and responsive to the needs of the people.

As the months passed, the sense of normalcy began to return. The nation's institutions were stronger, the public's confidence was slowly being restored, and the administration's efforts were yielding tangible results.

President Hayes, reflecting on the journey they had undertaken, felt a deep sense of responsibility and purpose. The battle against The Shadow Council had been a defining moment in his presidency, but it was also a reminder of the ongoing challenges of leadership.

In a conversation with General Lee, Hayes expressed his thoughts. "We've achieved a significant victory, but our work is far from over. The threat of corruption and tyranny is always present. We need to remain vigilant and committed to justice."

General Lee, with his characteristic resolve, replied, "We've faced incredible challenges, Mr. President, but we've also shown our strength and determination. We'll continue to fight for what's right and protect our nation."

Hayes nodded, feeling a sense of camaraderie and shared purpose. "We've come a long way, and we've demonstrated what we're capable of. The road ahead will be difficult, but we're ready to face it together."

As the administration continued its efforts to rebuild and strengthen the nation, the public's support and confidence grew. The sense of unity and resilience that had been forged in the crucible of conflict became a source of strength and inspiration.

President Hayes, reflecting on the lessons learned and the challenges of leadership, felt a renewed sense of purpose and determination. The battle against The Shadow Council had revealed the depth and complexity of the threats facing the nation, but it had also underscored the importance of integrity, vigilance, and unwavering commitment to justice.

In his final address to the nation on the subject, Hayes spoke with a sense of hope and resolve. "My fellow Americans, we have faced incredible challenges and made significant sacrifices, but we have emerged stronger. We have demonstrated our resilience, our unity, and our unwavering commitment to justice. As we move forward, let us remember the lessons we have learned and continue to build a nation that is strong, transparent, and accountable. Together, we will face the future with confidence and determination."

The journey was far from over, but with the strength and resolve of President Hayes and his team, the nation was in capable hands. The future was theirs to shape, and they were ready to face it with unwavering determination and a steadfast commitment to justice.

Chapter 15: A New Dawn

The sun rose over Washington, D.C., casting a golden light on the capital and signaling the beginning of a new day—a new era. President Daniel Hayes stood on the balcony of the White House, looking out over the city that had been the epicenter of a battle against corruption and tyranny. The immediate threat of The Shadow Council had been neutralized, but the journey of rebuilding and restoring trust was just beginning.

Inside the White House, the atmosphere was one of cautious optimism. The administration had faced and overcome incredible challenges, and now they were preparing to address the nation, to vow to rebuild and restore trust in the government. It was a moment of reflection and renewal, a time to honor the sacrifices made and to look to the future with hope and determination.

As Hayes prepared for his address, Olivia Barnes, his chief of staff, entered the room. She looked at the president with a mixture of pride and determination. "Mr. President, the nation is ready to hear from you. They need to hear your vision for the future, to understand how we will rebuild and move forward."

Hayes nodded, feeling the weight of the moment. "It's time to turn the page, Olivia. We've faced dark times, but we've also shown our strength and resilience. This is our chance to chart a new course, to ensure that we build a government that is transparent, accountable, and worthy of the public's trust."

The president walked to the podium in the East Room, where a large audience had gathered, including government officials, military leaders, and families of the fallen. The room was filled with a sense of anticipation and hope. As the cameras rolled and the broadcast began, Hayes took a deep breath and began his address.

"My fellow Americans," he began, his voice steady and resonant, "we have faced unprecedented challenges and made significant sacrifices. The battle against The Shadow Council tested our resolve and our strength, but it also revealed the depth of our commitment to justice and democracy. Today, we stand at the dawn of a new era, determined to rebuild and restore trust in our government."

Hayes paused, his eyes scanning the room and the cameras, connecting with the nation. "We honor the bravery and sacrifice of those who gave their lives to protect our freedoms. Their courage has ensured our safety and preserved our democracy. We owe them a debt of gratitude, and we vow to continue their fight."

The president's words resonated deeply with the audience, and a ripple of applause filled the room. Hayes continued, outlining his vision for the future.

"We are committed to creating a government that is transparent, accountable, and responsive to the needs of the people. We will strengthen our institutions, enhance our security, and ensure that those who seek to harm us are brought to justice. We will implement new policies and reforms to prevent corruption and build a government that is worthy of your trust."

As Hayes spoke, he felt a sense of unity and resolve in the room. The nation had been through a crucible, but it had emerged stronger and more resilient. The public's confidence was slowly being restored, and the administration's efforts were yielding tangible results.

"In the coming months, we will focus on rebuilding our infrastructure, supporting our economy, and ensuring that our institutions are strong and resilient. We will work to restore public trust and confidence, and we will remain vigilant in protecting our democracy. Together, we will face the future with hope and determination."

Hayes concluded his address with a message of hope and resilience. "We have faced dark times, but we have also shown our strength and our commitment to justice. As we move forward, let us remember the lessons we have learned and continue to build a nation that is strong, transparent, and accountable. Together, we will face the future with confidence and determination."

The audience erupted in applause, and the sense of hope and unity was palpable. The address marked a turning point, a moment of renewal and determination. The nation was ready to rebuild and move forward, guided by a sense of purpose and resolve.

In the days that followed, the administration focused on implementing their plans for rebuilding and restoring trust. They conducted a thorough review of security protocols, identified areas for improvement, and implemented new measures to prevent future threats. The focus was on creating a government that was transparent, accountable, and responsive to the needs of the people.

The administration also launched initiatives to support the families of those who had fallen in the fight against The Shadow Council. They provided financial assistance, counseling, and support services to help them rebuild their lives and honor the memory of their loved ones.

One evening, as President Hayes reflected on the journey they had undertaken, he sat down with Olivia, General Marcus Lee, and Rachel Wu to discuss their progress and the road ahead.

"We've come a long way," Hayes began, his voice filled with a sense of accomplishment. "But we still have much work to do. The public's trust is slowly being restored, and our institutions are becoming stronger. We need to continue our efforts and remain vigilant."

Olivia nodded, her expression thoughtful. "We've made significant progress, but the threat of corruption is always present. We need to ensure that our reforms are comprehensive and that we build systems that are resilient and transparent."

General Lee added, "Our security measures are stronger than ever, but we must remain proactive. The battle against The Shadow Council has shown us the importance of vigilance and preparedness. We need to stay ahead of potential threats and ensure that we are always ready to respond."

Rachel Wu spoke up, her voice filled with determination. "Our cybersecurity efforts have made a significant impact, but we need to continue to innovate and adapt. The threat landscape is constantly evolving, and we need to ensure that our defenses are always one step ahead."

The conversation was a reminder of the ongoing challenges they faced, but it was also a testament to their resolve and commitment. The administration's efforts were yielding results, and the sense of hope and determination was palpable.

As the months passed, the nation continued to heal and rebuild. The public's confidence grew, and the sense of unity and resilience that had been forged in the face of adversity became a source of strength and inspiration. The administration's focus on transparency, accountability, and reform resonated deeply with the people, and the sense of trust and confidence was slowly being restored.

President Hayes, reflecting on the journey they had undertaken, felt a deep sense of responsibility and purpose. The battle against The Shadow Council had been a defining moment in his presidency, but it was also a reminder of the ongoing challenges of leadership. The fight against corruption and tyranny was far from over, but the nation was stronger and more resilient than ever.

In a conversation with General Lee, Hayes expressed his thoughts. "We've achieved a significant victory, but our work is far from over. The threat of corruption and tyranny is always present. We need to remain vigilant and committed to justice."

General Lee, with his characteristic resolve, replied, "We've faced incredible challenges, Mr. President, but we've also shown our strength and determination. We'll continue to fight for what's right and protect our nation."

Hayes nodded, feeling a sense of camaraderie and shared purpose. "We've come a long way, and we've demonstrated what we're capable of. The road ahead will be difficult, but we're ready to face it together."

As the administration continued its efforts to rebuild and strengthen the nation, the public's support and confidence grew. The sense of unity and resilience that had been forged in the crucible of conflict became a source of strength and inspiration.

President Hayes, reflecting on the lessons learned and the challenges of leadership, felt a renewed sense of purpose and determination. The battle against The Shadow Council had revealed the depth and complexity of the threats facing the nation, but it had also underscored the importance of integrity, vigilance, and unwavering commitment to justice.

In his final address to the nation on the subject, Hayes spoke with a sense of hope and resolve. "My fellow Americans, we have faced incredible challenges and made significant sacrifices, but we have emerged stronger. We have demonstrated our resilience, our unity, and our unwavering commitment to justice. As we move forward, let us remember the lessons we have learned and continue to build a nation that is strong, transparent, and accountable. Together, we will face the future with confidence and determination."

The journey was far from over, but with the strength and resolve of President Hayes and his team, the nation was in capable hands. The future was theirs to shape, and they were ready to face it with unwavering determination and a steadfast commitment to justice.

As the administration continued its efforts to dismantle The Shadow Council's network, they remained vigilant and proactive. The enemy was cunning and resilient, but the administration's determination and resolve were unwavering.

One evening, as President Hayes sat in the Oval Office reflecting on the progress they had made, Olivia entered with a determined look on her face.

"Mr. President, we've identified another key operative within The Shadow Council," she said, handing him a report. "This operative has been coordinating the disinformation campaign and is responsible for many of the cyberattacks we've faced."

Hayes felt a surge of determination. "We need to take them down. What's the plan?"

Olivia outlined the operation, which involved a coordinated effort between cyber operatives and field agents. Rachel Wu would lead the cyber aspect, using advanced techniques to breach the operative's digital defenses and gather critical intelligence. John Carter's team would handle the physical apprehension, conducting a raid to capture the operative and secure any evidence.

The operation was meticulously planned and executed. Rachel's team launched a cyberattack to disrupt the operative's communications and coordination, while John's team moved in to apprehend the target. The raid was a success, resulting in the capture of the operative and the seizure of critical evidence.

The captured operative provided valuable intelligence, revealing more about The Shadow Council's operations and plans. The administration used this intelligence to launch further operations, disrupting key activities and weakening the network's hold.

Despite the successes, the fight was far from over. The Shadow Council continued to adapt and evolve, using their resources and influence to mount new attacks and spread disinformation. The administration had to remain vigilant and proactive, constantly adjusting their strategies to stay ahead of the enemy.

As the weeks passed, the team's efforts began to yield significant results. The public started to see the administration's determination and resilience, and confidence slowly began to return. The stock market stabilized, and financial institutions resumed normal operations. Power grids were secured, and communication networks were restored.

President Hayes addressed the nation once again, his tone resolute and hopeful. "My fellow Americans, we have faced an unprecedented challenge, but we have stood strong. Our efforts to dismantle The Shadow Council's network are yielding results, and we are restoring stability and security. We will continue to fight for the integrity of our nation and the trust of our people. Together, we will emerge from this stronger and more united."

The administration's efforts were recognized and celebrated, and President Hayes emerged as a symbol of integrity and resilience. The fight against The Shadow Council had tested their resolve, but it had also strengthened their commitment to justice and the values that defined their nation.

As the administration continued its efforts to protect the nation and restore public trust, President Hayes knew that the journey was far from over. The fight against corruption and betrayal would be ongoing, but with the support of a dedicated team and the determination to see it through, they would prevail.

The shadows of The Shadow Council had been exposed, and the path ahead was clear. Together, they had faced the darkness and emerged victorious, and the future was bright with the promise of justice and integrity.

The presidency was a heavy burden, but it was one that Hayes bore with honor and a deep sense of responsibility. The challenges had been immense, but they had demonstrated their commitment to justice and the values that defined their nation. The journey was far from over, but with each step, they moved closer to building a brighter and more secure future.

The betrayal had been unveiled, and the fight against corruption continued. But with the strength and resolve of President Hayes and his team, the nation was in capable hands. The future was theirs to shape, and they were ready to face it with unwavering determination and a steadfast commitment to justice.

Don't miss out!

Visit the website below and you can sign up to receive emails whenever Nicholas Andrew Martinez publishes a new book. There's no charge and no obligation.

https://books2read.com/r/B-A-HUIXB-RMXIF

BOOKS 2 READ

Connecting independent readers to independent writers.

About the Author

Nicholas Andrew Martinez is a distinguished author known for his gripping political fiction. His novels delve into the intricacies of power, corruption, and intrigue, offering readers a thrilling and insightful look at the political landscape. With a background in political science and a passion for storytelling, Martinez crafts narratives that are both thought-provoking and suspenseful. Outside of writing, he enjoys analyzing current events, traveling, and engaging in civic discussions. Nicholas's work continues to captivate and challenge readers, cementing his reputation as a leading voice in political fiction.

9 798230 998419